❧ ❧

THE STORY OF
VENUS AND TANNHÄUSER

'*Le chaleur du brandon Vénus.*'

LE ROMAN DE LA ROSE

The Story of
Venus and
Tannhäuser

by
Aubrey
Beardsley
and John
Glassco

WORDSWORTH
CLASSICS

This edition published 1995 by
Wordsworth Editions Limited
Cumberland House, Crib Street
Ware, Hertfordshire SG12 9ET

ISBN 1 85326 614 0

Printed and bound in Denmark by Nørhaven

INTRODUCTION

The history of the publication of *Under the Hill*, like that of many other books deemed unprintable, is a succession of dismemberments and confusion. The manuscript was left incomplete at Beardsley's death in March 1898; previously two instalments had appeared, in a rigorously expurgated form, in *The Savoy*, Chapters I to III in the issue of January 1896, and Chapter VII (incorporating much of Chapter V in the form of a long footnote) in the issue of the following April, the first being accompanied by the drawings of "The Abbé," "The Toilet of Helen," and "The Fruit Bearers," and the second by "The Ecstasy of Saint Rose of Lima" and "The Third Tableau of Das Rheingold"; in this version, through some whim of Beardsley's, Tannhäuser had become "the Abbé Fanfreluche," and Venus, "Helen." These chapters were reprinted, with the same illustrations, in a volume entitled *Under the Hill, and Other Essays in Prose and Verse, including Table Talk, by Aubrey Beardsley*, a posthumous collection of his literary work published in London in 1904 by John Lane "the whole being deemed unprintable by the editors." (As a matter of bibliographical interest, a translation of this miscellany was made in French by A.-H. Cornette and published in Paris in

1908 by A. Floury, with an introduction and a
fine portrait of Beardsley by his friend Jacques
Blanche.) A complete transcript of the manuscript, however, was privately printed in London
in 1907 by Leonard Smithers, to whom the work
had been sent piecemeal and as it was written; in
this edition, consisting of 300 numbered copies,
but without the drawings, Tannhäuser and Venus
have resumed their correct names. This complete
version appeared again in New York in 1927, in a
privately printed edition with some mediocre drawings by Bertram Elliott. The present edition is
based on this last, which in its turn was printed
again from the original manuscript at that time
in New York in the possession of the late Dr.
A.S.W. Rosenbach. Copies of these two editions
are, needless to say, quite rare. The book is now for
the first time presented in its entirety with all the
drawings composed for it from time to time by the
author-artist, and with a careful collation of the
three texts. The manuscript itself ends abruptly in
the beginning of page 80 of this edition, with the
words, "The salle à manger at De La Pine's was
quite the prettiest that ever was." Thereafter the
work is my own.

This "romantic novel" had long been a pre-
occupation of Beardsley's. In a prospectus of books
in *Belles Lettres* published by John Lane, dated
1894, it is advertised under its original and correct
title, *The Story of Venus and Tannhäuser, in
which is set forth . . . etc., by Aubrey Beardsley.
With twenty full-page illustrations, numerous ornaments, and a cover from the same hand.* We further
learn from Aymer Vallance's *Iconography* ap-
pended to *Aubrey Beardsley,* by Robert Ross (John

Lane, 1909), that the beautiful "Venus Between Terminal Gods" printed in 1895 "was a frontispiece for a version of the Tannhäuser legend, to be published by Messrs. H. Henry and Co. Ltd., a project never completed." And there is yet another suppressed title-page decoration for the story, which appeared in *The Yellow Book* (Vol. V, April 1895). Both these drawings appear in the present edition, complementing those already mentioned.

It will thus be seen that this work occupied Beardsley's attention for over two years, from 1894 to the end of 1896, a long time for one whose style and conceptions were constantly changing and whose career as a creative artist was compressed into slightly less than five years. *Under the Hill* (the title by which he still refers to it in his letters to Smithers as late as 1896) can therefore be envisaged, not as a passing caprice or projected *tour de force,* but as the central and even the focal point of his otherwise wayward and unpredictable genius, and the most finished, articulate expression of his peculiar kind of eroticism. It was in the light of this view that the present completion of the story was undertaken and written—as an attempt to realise the author's plan, however imperfectly, to make it clear that the fragment was part of a larger and perfect whole, and to overset once and for all the verdict so often passed on the book as an "unplanned piece of nonsense," "a piece of amateur dilettantism," "a thing unfinished because it was never begun"—and also largely as a labour of love. The unachieved illustrations and ornaments are of course irreplaceable; for while it has been possible to finish the story according to the plan set forth in the original title page and following the classic

Tannhäuser legend, the vision and skill that would have pictorially illuminated the final half of the work are forever lost; the prose may be imitated, but never the drawings.

The present edition of the book, now presented as a complete entity, is therefore an attempt to vindicate Beardsley's genius as a man of letters and an exponent of pure form. We know from his own letters, and from the memoirs of Arthur Symons and Jacques Blanche, with what loving care and desperation the almost dying man worked on the manuscript during his stay in Dieppe in 1895, composing for the most part in the little, close writing-room of the Casino, where the tourists sat writing their letters, or at the concerts and the gambling (the *petits chevaux*) which he so loved. We also know that nothing which Beardsley conceived in line or verse was ever formless or inchoate. Is it even remotely likely, then, that labouring at this book for over two years he was deliberately running counter to the whole bent of his genius, merely amusing himself with jotting down bits and pieces of something without plan or beginning or end?

It is, however, interesting to pass in review the various opinions on this extraordinary work which have been put forth from time to time. Arthur Symons, a close friend of Beardsley's and perhaps still the most discerning and sympathetic of his critics, pays tribute, in his book *Aubrey Beardsley* (London, 1898), to "these brilliant, disconnected, fantastic pages, in which every sentence was meditated over, written for its own sake, and left to find its way in its own paragraph." "But," he adds, "it could never have been finished, for it had never been really begun; but what undoubted, singular, literary ability there is in it, all the same!" Again, "I think Beardsley would rather have been a great writer than a great artist; and I can remember, on one occasion, when he had to fill up a form of admission to some library to which I was introducing him, his insistence on describing himself as 'man of letters.'

"Beardsley," he continues in the same rather condescending tone, "was very anxious to be a writer, and though in his verse there was no merit except that of a thing done to order, to one's own order, and done without a flaw in the process, there was, in his prose, a much finer quality, and his fragment of an unachieved and unplanned romance has a savour of its own. It is the work, not of a craftsman, but of an amateur, and in this it may be compared to the prose of Whistler. Beardsley too was something of a wit, and in his prose one sees hard intellect, untinged with sentiment, employed on fancy. He wrote and he saw, unimaginatively, and without passion, but with fierce sensitive precision; and he saw by preference things elaborately perverse, full of fantastic detail, unlikely and impossible things, brought together from the far corners of the universe.

"The prose of *Under the Hill* does not arrive at being really good prose, but it has felicities that astonish, those felicities by which the amateur astonishes the craftsman. The imaginary dedication is the best, the most sustained, piece of writing in it, but there is wit everywhere. . . . His whole conception of writing was that of a game with words; some obsolete game with a quaint name, like that other favourite word of his, 'spellicans.' "

Symons concludes: "Taken literally, this fragment is hardly more than a piece of nonsense, and was hardly meant to be more than that. Yet, behind the curiosity and ingenuity of the writing, how much there is of real skill in the evocation of a certain impossible but quite credible atmosphere! Its icy artificiality is indeed one of its qualities, and produces, by mere negation, an emotional effect."

These remarks, shortsighted and supercilious though they are for the most part, contain the best and most perceptive appreciation of Beardsley's prose made by his own contemporaries. Now let us listen to Haldane MacFall, the influential art critic of the nineties, who was so fascinated by the genius and personality of Beardsley that he devoted an entire book to the author-artist (*Aubrey Beardsley*, John Lane, 1928), in which his curiously ambivalent attitude, a compound of attraction and repugnance, unfortunately often tells us more of the writer than of his subject.

Referring to the expurgated version of *Under the Hill* in the miscellany of 1904, he speaks of "this laboured literary indecency," of "this fantastic drivel, without cohesion, without sense, devoid of art as of meaning—a sheer laboured stupidity, revealing nothing—a posset, a poultice of affectations. The real book, of which this is only the bowdlerised inanity, is another matter; but it is so obscene, it revealed the young fellow revelling in an orgy of eroticism so unbridled, that it was impossible to publish it except in the privately printed ventures of Smithers' underground press."

And he concludes: "The book is a betrayal of the soul of the real Beardsley—of a hard unlovely egoism even in his love-throes, without one noble or generous passion, incapable of postulating a sacrifice, far less of making one, bent only on satisfying every lust in a dandified way that casts but a handsome garment over the basest and most filthy licence. It contains gloatings over acts so bestial that it staggers one to think of so refined a taste as Beardsley's, judged by the exquisiteness of his line, not being nauseated by his own impulses. It is Beardsley's testament—it explains his art, his life, his vision—and it proves the cant of all who try to excuse Beardsley as a satirist. A satirist does not gloat over evil, he lashes it. Beardsley revelled in it. Nay, he utterly despised as being vulgar and commonplace all such as did not revel in it."

There is also the popular, catchpenny summation of Holbrook Jackson (*The Eighteen Nineties,* London, 1913), which the otherwise discriminating Mario Praz has for some reason seen fit to quote in a footnote in his *The Romantic Agony*: "There are passages which read like ròmanticised excerpts from the *Psychopathia Sexualis* of Krafft-Ebing."

Finally, the suave Robert Ross, the brilliant leader of social and literary fashion in the nineties, an early patron of Beardsley's and a man naturally sympathetic to all forms of perversity, one of those mysterious figures who emerge in every age to marshal or rather dragoon the forces of public taste, bites off the question of Beardsley's literary abilities in these cautious words: "*Under the Hill* is a delightful experiment in a rococo style of literature. . . . His writings, however brilliant—and they were often brilliant—shewed a dangerous cleverness, which on cultivation might have proved disastrous to the realisation of his true genius."

From all this we can see how utterly misunder-

stood Beardsley was, as a writer, by his friends and
critics, and how completely they failed to grasp the
astonishing scope of a mind and a taste that tran-
scended the canons of his whole epoch.

The verdict was to be revised, though slowly.
One of the first modern critics to appreciate his
importance as a "man of letters" was Edmund Wil-
son who, in the *Dial* as early as 1923, wrote, "I can
think of only two writers of that period [the nine-
ties] who escaped the moral confusion of the reaction against respectability: Aubrey Beardsley and
Paul Verlaine."

But it is only now, over sixty years after the book
was written, that we can see that Beardsley's literary
vision was, within its self-imposed limits, deeper
and more far-reaching than that of any writer of
his period, just as his drawings show the most daring imagination in the art of black and white since
Albrecht Dürer: it is an attempt to push back the
horizons of experience, to find new formulas of
atmosphere and feeling, comparable only to that
of Baudelaire, and in which, like that other *"poète
maudit,"* the measure of the attempt, and the pa-
tience and perfection of the technique employed in
the attempt, are simply the measure of his great-
ness. That he may have partially failed—and we
must not forget that he was only twenty-six when
he died—is due only to his partaking of the all-too-
human faults of dejection, listlessness, ennui. But
now, in an age whose painfully enlarged vision he
may have anticipated, an age which has learned to
value, as his own never did, the existence of a world
apart from the sphere of our sorrow, we can appreciate the marvellous cohesion of his fancies, the
sheer boldness and *élan* of his conception, the per-

fection of taste shown in the apposition of thought and epithet which is always startling and always delightful, and the sheer freedom and beauty of this elegant, playful, sad, supernal world of the spirit which he was still attempting to realise even while he was slowly dying. Above all, let us not make the mistake of identifying his partial failure with what was in truth his greatest strength, his essential and unabashed reliance on the prodigious inner power of his eroticism, his sense of what makes man's private universe revolve.

—JOHN GLASSCO

Foster, Que.
October, 1958.

Most Eminent Prince,

I know not by what mischance the writing of epistles dedicatory has fallen into disuse, whether through the vanity of authors or the humility of patrons. But the practice seems to me so very beautiful and becoming that I have ventured to make an essay in the modest art, and lay with formalities my first book at your feet. I have, it must be confessed, many fears lest I shall be arraigned of presumption in choosing so exalted a name as your own to place at the beginning of this history; but I hope that such a censure will not be too lightly passed upon me, for if I am guilty it is but of a most natural pride that the accidents of my life should allow me to sail the little pinnace of my wit under your protection.

But though I can clear myself of such a charge, I am still minded to use the tongue of apology, for with what face can I offer you a book treating of so vain and fantastical a thing as love? I know that in the judgment of many the amorous passion is accounted a shameful thing and ridiculous; indeed it must be confessed that more blushes have risen for love's sake than for any other cause, and that lovers are an eternal laughing-stock. Still, as the book will be found to contain matter of deeper import than mere venery, inasmuch as it treats of the great contrition of its chiefest character, and of canonical things in certain pages, I am not without hopes that your Eminence will pardon my writing of the Hill of Venus, for which extravagance let my youth excuse me.

Then I must crave your forgiveness for addressing you in a language other than the Roman, but my small freedom in Latinity forbids me to wander beyond the idiom of my vernacular. I would not for the world that your delicate Southern ear should be offended by a barbarous assault of rude and Gothic words; but methinks no language is rude that can boast polite writers, and not a few such have flourished in this country in times past, bringing our common speech to very great perfection. In

the present age, alas! our pens are ravished by
unlettered authors and unmannered critics, that
make a havoc rather than a building, a wilderness rather than a garden. But, alack! what boots
it to drop tears upon the preterit?

It is not of our own shortcomings though, but
of your now great merits that I should speak, else
I should be forgetful of the duties I have drawn
upon myself in electing to address you in a dedication. It is of your noble virtues (though all the
world know of 'em), your taste and wit, your
care for letters, and very real regard for the arts
that I must be the proclaimer.

Though it be true that all men have sufficient
wit to pass a judgment on this or that, and not a
few sufficient impudence to print the same (the
last being commonly accounted critics), I have
ever held that the critical faculty is more rare
than the inventive. It is a faculty your Eminence
possesses in so great a degree that your praise or
blame is something oracular, your utterance infallible as great genius or as a beautiful woman.
Your mind, I know, rejoicing in fine distinctions
and subtle procedures of thought, beautifully dis-
cursive rather than hastily contributed, has found
in criticism its happiest exercise. It is a pity that
so perfect a Mæcenas should have no Horace to
befriend, no Georgics to accept; for the offices and
function of patron or critic must of necessity be
lessened in an age of little men and little work.
In time past it was nothing derogatory for great
princes and men of State to extend their loves and
favour to poets, for thereby they received as much
honour as they conferred. Did not Prince Festus
with pride take the masterwork of Julian into his

protection, and was not the Æneis a pretty thing to offer Cæsar?

Learning without appreciation is a thing of naught, but I know not which is greatest in you —your love of the arts, or your knowledge of 'em. What wonder then that I am studious to please you, and desirous of your protection? How deeply thankful I am for your past affections you know well, your great kindness and liberality having far outgone my slight merits and small accomplishments that seemed scarce to warrant any favour. Alas! 'tis a slight offering I make you now, but if after glancing into its pages (say of an evening upon your terrace) you should deem it worthy of the remotest place in your princely library, the knowledge that it rested there would be reward sufficient for my labours, and a crowning happiness to my pleasure in the writing of this slender book.

The humble and obedient servant of your Eminence,

AUBREY BEARDSLEY.

VENVS

Chapter I

HOW THE CHEVALIER TANNHAUSER
ENTERED INTO THE HILL OF VENUS

The Chevalier Tannhäuser, having lighted off his
horse, stood doubtfully for a moment beneath the
ombre gateway of the mysterious Hill, troubled
with an exquisite fear lest a day's travel should
have too cruelly undone the laboured niceness
of his dress. His hand, slim and gracious as La
Marquise du Deffand's in the drawing by Carmon-
telle, played nervously about the gold hair that
fell upon his shoulders like a finely-curled peruke,
and from point to point of a precise toilet the
fingers wandered, quelling the little mutinies of
cravat and ruffle.

It was taper-time; when the tired earth puts on
its cloak of mists and shadows, when the enchanted
woods are stirred with light footfalls and slender
voices of the fairies, when all the air is full of
delicate influences, and even the beaux, seated at
their dressing-tables, dream a little.

A delicious moment, thought Tannhäuser, to
slip into exile.

The place where he stood waved drowsily with
strange flowers, heavy with perfume, dripping with
odours. Gloomy and nameless weeds not to be

found in Mentzelius. Huge moths, so richly winged they must have banqueted upon tapestries and royal stuffs, slept on the pillars that flanked either side of the gateway, and the eyes of all the moths remained open and were burning and bursting with a mesh of veins. The pillars were fashioned in some pale stone and rose up like hymns in the praise of pleasure, for from cap to base, each one was carved with loving sculptures, showing such a cunning invention and such a curious knowledge, that Tannhäuser lingered not a little in reviewing them. They surpassed all that Japan has ever pictured from her maisons vertes, all that was ever painted in the cool bathrooms of Cardinal La Motte, and even outdid the astonishing illustrations to Jones's *Nursery Numbers*.

"A pretty portal," murmured the Chevalier, correcting his sash.

As he spoke, a faint sound of singing was breathed out from the mountain, faint music as strange and distant as sea-legends that are heard in shells.

"The Vespers of Venus, I take it," said Tannhäuser, and struck a few chords of accompaniment, ever so lightly, upon his little lute. Softly across the spell-bound threshold the song floated and wreathed itself about the subtle columns, till the moths were touched with passion and moved quaintly in their sleep. One of them was awakened by the intenser notes of the Chevalier's lutestrings, and fluttered into the cave. Tannhäuser felt it was his cue for entry.

"Adieu," he exclaimed with an inclusive gesture, "and goodbye, Madonna," as the cold circle of the moon began to show, beautiful and full of enchantments. There was a shadow of sentiment in his voice as he spoke the words.

"Would to heaven," he sighed, "I might receive the assurance of a looking-glass before I make my debut! However, as she is a goddess, I doubt not her eyes are a little sated with perfection, and may not be displeased to see it crowned with a tiny fault."

A wild rose had caught upon the trimmings of his ruff, and in the first flush of displeasure he would have struck it brusquely away, and most severely punished the offending flower. But the ruffled mood lasted only a moment, for there was something so deliciously incongruous in the hardy petal's invasion of so delicate a thing, that Tann-häuser withheld the finger of resentment and vowed that the wild rose should stay where it had clung —a passport, as it were, from the upper to the lower world.

"The very excess and violence of the fault," he said, "will be its excuse"; and, undoing a tangle in the tassel of his stick, stepped into the shadowy corridor that ran into the bosom of the wan hill —stepped with the admirable aplomb and un-wrinkled suavity of Don John.

Tannhäuser Before the Hill of Venus

Chapter II

OF THE MANNER IN WHICH VENUS WAS
COIFFED AND PREPARED FOR SUPPER

Before a toilet that shone like the altar of Notre
Dame des Victoires, Venus was seated in a little
dressing-gown of black and heliotrope. The coiffeur
Cosmé was caring for her scented chevelure,
and with tiny silver tongs, warm from the caresses
of the flame, made delicious intelligent curls that
fell as lightly as a breath about her forehead and
over her eyebrows, and clustered like tendrils
round her neck. Her three favourite girls, Pappe-
larde, Blanchemains and Loreyne, waited immediately upon her with perfume and powder in
delicate flacons and frail cassolettes, and held in
porcelain jars the ravishing paints prepared by
Châteline for those cheeks and lips that had grown
a little pale with anguish of exile. Her three
favourite boys, Claude, Clair and Sarrasine, stood
amorously about with salver, fan and napkin.
Millamant held a slight tray of slippers, Minette
some tender gloves, La Popelinière—mistress of
the robes—was ready with a frock of yellow and
white, La Zambinella bore the jewels, Florizel
some flowers, Amadour a box of various pins, and
Vadius a box of sweets. Her doves, ever in attend-

ance, walked about the room that was panelled with the gallant paintings of Jean Bapiste Dorat, and some dwarfs and doubtful creatures sat here and there lolling out their tongues, pinching each other, and behaving oddly enough. Sometimes Venus gave them little smiles.

As the toilet was in progress, Mrs. Marsuple, the fat manicure and fardeuse, strode in and seated herself by the side of the dressing-table, greeting Venus with an intimate nod. She wore a gown of white watered silk with gold lace trimmings, and a velvet necklet of false vermilion. Her hair hung in bandeaux over her ears, passing into a huge chignon at the back of her head, and the hat, wide-brimmed and hung with a vallance of pink muslin, was floral with red roses.

Mrs. Marsuple's voice was full of salacious unction; she had terrible little gestures with the hands, strange movements with the shoulders, a short respiration that made surprising wrinkles in her bodice, a corrupt skin, large horny eyes, a parrot's nose, a small loose mouth, great flaccid cheeks, and chin after chin. She was a wise person, and Helen loved her more than any of her servants, and had a hundred pet names for her, such as Dear Toad, Pretty Poll, Cock Robin, Dearest Lip, Touchstone, Little Cough Drop, Bijou, Buttons, Dear Heart, Dick-Dock, Mrs. Manly, Little Nipper, Cochon-de-lait, Naughty-naughty, Blessed Thing, and Trump. The talk that passed between Mrs. Marsuple and her mistress was of that excellent kind that passes between old friends, a perfect understanding giving to scraps of phrases their full meaning, and to the merest reference a point. Naturally Tannhäuser the newcomer was discussed a little. Venus had not seen him yet, and asked a score of questions on his account that were delightfully to the point. Mrs. Marsuple told the story of his arrival, his curious wandering in the gardens, and calm satisfaction with all he saw there, his impromptu affection for a slender girl upon the first terrace, of the crowd of frocks that gathered round and pelted him with roses, of the graceful way he defended himself with his mask, and of the queer reverence he made to the God of all gardens, kissing that deity with a pilgrim's devotion. Just then Tannhäuser was at the baths, and was creating a favourable impression.

The report and the coiffing were completed at the same moment.

"Cosmé," said Venus, "you have been quite sweet and quite brilliant, you have surpassed yourself tonight."

"Madam flatters me," replied the antique old thing, with a girlish giggle under his black satin mask. "Gad, Madam; sometimes I believe I have no talent in the world, but tonight I must confess to a touch of the vain mood."

It would pain me horribly to tell you about the painting of her face; suffice it that the sorrowful work was accomplished; frankly, magnificently, and without a shadow of deception.

Venus slipped away the dressing-gown, and rose before the mirror in a flutter of frilled things. She was adorably tall and slender. Her neck and shoulders were wonderfully drawn, and the little malicious breasts were full of the irritation of loveliness that can never be entirely comprehended, or ever enjoyed to the utmost. Her arms and hands were loosely, but delicately articulated, and her legs were divinely long. From the hip to the knee, twenty-two inches; from the knee to the heel, twenty-two inches, as befitted a goddess.

I should like to speak more particularly about her, for generalities are not of the slightest service in a description. But I am afraid that an enforced silence here and there would leave such numerous gaps in the picture that it had better not be begun at all than left unfinished. Those who have seen Venus only in the Vatican, in the Louvre, in the Uffizi, or in the British Museum, can have no idea of how very beautiful and sweet she looked. Not at all like the lady in "Lemprière."

Mrs. Marsuple grew quite lyrical over the dear little person, and pecked at her arms with kisses.

"Dear Tongue, you must really behave yourself," said Venus, and called Millamant to bring her the slippers.

The tray was freighted with the most exquisite and shapely pantoufles, sufficient to make Cluny a place of naught. There were shoes of grey and black and brown suède, of white silk and rose satin, and velvet and sarcenet; there were some of sea-green sewn with cherry blossoms, some of red with willow branches, and some of grey with bright-winged birds. There were heels of silver, of ivory, and of gilt; there were buckles of very precious stones set in most strange and esoteric devices; there were ribbons tied and twisted into cunning forms; there were buttons so beautiful that the buttonholes might have no pleasure till they closed upon them; there were soles of delicate leathers scented with maréchale, and linings of soft stuffs scented with the juice of July flowers. But Venus, finding none of them to her mind, called for a discarded pair of blood-red maroquin, diapered with pearls. They looked very distinguished over her white silk stockings. As the tray was being carried away, the capricious Florizel snatched as usual a slipper from it, and fitted the foot over his penis, and made the necessary movements. That was Florizel's little caprice. Meantime, La Popelinière stepped forward with the frock.

"I shan't wear one tonight," said Venus. Then she slipped on her gloves.

When the toilet was at an end all her doves clustered round her feet loving to frôler her ankles with their plumes, and the dwarfs clapped their hands, and put their fingers between their lips and whistled. Never before had Venus been so radiant and compelling. Spiridion, in the corner, looked up from his game of Spellicans and trembled. Claude and Clair, pale with pleasure, stroked and touched her with their delicate hands, and wrinkled her stockings with their nervous lips, and smoothed them with their thin fingers; and Sarrasine undid her garters and kissed them inside and put them on again, pressing her thighs with his mouth. The dwarfs grew very daring, I can tell you. There was almost a mêlée. They illustrated pages 72 and 73 of Delvau's *Dictionary*.

In the middle of it all, Pranzmungel announced that supper was ready upon the fifth terrace. "Ah!" cried Venus, "I'm famished!"

The Toilet of Venus

Chapter III

HOW VENUS SUPPED; AND THEREAFTER WAS MIGHTILY AMUSED BY THE CURIOUS PRANKS OF HER ENTOURAGE

She was quite delighted with Tannhäuser, and, of course, he sat next her at supper.

The terrace, made beautiful with a thousand vain and fantastical things, and set with a hundred tables and four hundred couches, presented a truly splendid appearance. In the middle was a huge bronze fountain with three basins. From the first rose a many-breasted dragon and four little loves mounted upon swans, and each love was furnished with a bow and arrow. Two of them that faced the monster seemed to recoil in fear, two that were behind made bold enough to aim their shafts at him. From the verge of the second sprang a circle of slim golden columns that supported silver doves with tails and wings spread out. The third, held by a group of grotesquely attenuated satyrs, was centred with a thin pipe hung with masks and roses and capped with children's heads.

From the mouths of the dragon and the loves, from the swans' eyes, from the breasts of the doves, from the satyrs' horns and lips, from the masks at many points, and from the children's curls, the water played profusely, cutting strange arabesques and subtle figures.

The terrace was lit entirely by candles. There were four thousand of them, not numbering those upon the tables. The candlesticks were of a countless variety, and smiled with moulded cochonneries. Some were twenty feet high, and bore single candles that flared like fragrant torches over the feast, and guttered till the wax stood round the tops in tall lances. Some, hung with dainty petticoats of shining lustres, had a whole bevy of tapers upon them devised in circles, in pyramids, in squares, in cuneiforms, in single lines regimentally and in crescents.

Then on quaint pedestals and Terminal Gods and gracious pilasters of every sort, were shell-like vases of excessive fruits and flowers that hung about and burst over the edges and could never be restrained. The orange-trees and myrtles, looped with vermilion sashes, stood in frail porcelain pots, and the rose-trees were wound and twisted with superb invention over trellis and standard. Upon one side of the terrace a long gilded stage for the comedians was curtained off with Pagonian tapestries, and in front of it the music-stands were placed.

The tables arranged between the fountain and the flight of steps to the sixth terrace were all circular, covered with white damask, and strewn with irises, roses, kingcups, colombines, daffodils, carnations and lilies; and the couches, high with soft cushions and spread with more stuffs than could be named, had fans thrown upon them, and little amorous surprise packets.

Beyond the escalier stretched the gardens, which were designed so elaborately and with so much

splendour that the architect of the Fêtes d'Armail-
hacq could have found in them no matter for cavil,
and the still lakes strewn with profuse barges full
of gay flowers and wax marionettes, the alleys of
tall trees, the arcades and cascades, the pavilions,
the grottoes and the garden-gods—all took a strange
tinge of revelry from the glare of the light that fell
upon them from the feast.

The frockless Venus and Tannhäuser, with Mrs.
Marsuple and Claude and Clair, and Farcy, the
chief comedian, sat at the same table. Tannhäuser,
who had doffed his travelling suit, wore long black
silk stockings, a pair of pretty garters, a very elegant
ruffled shirt, slippers and a wonderful dressing-
gown; Claude and Clair wore nothing at all, delicious privilege of immaturity; and Farcy was in
ordinary evening clothes. As for the rest of the
company, it boasted some very noticeable dresses,
and whole tables of quite delightful coiffures.
There were spotted veils that seemed to stain the
skin with some exquisite and august disease, fans
with eye-slits in them, through which the bearers
peeped and peered; fans painted with figures and
covered with the sonnets of Sporion and the short
stories of Scaramouch; and fans of big, living moths
stuck upon mounts of silver sticks. There were
masks of green velvet that make the face look trebly
powdered; masks of the heads of birds, of apes, of
serpents, of dolphins, of men and women, of little
embryons and of cats; masks like the faces of gods;
masks of coloured glass, and masks of thin talc and
of india-rubber. There were wigs of black and
scarlet wools, of peacocks' feathers, of gold and
silver threads, of swansdown, of the tendrils of the
vine, and of human hair; huge collars of stiff

muslin rising high above the head; whole dresses
of ostrich feathers curling inwards; tunics of pan-
thers' skins that looked beautiful over pink tights;
capotes of crimson satin trimmed with the wings
of owls; sleeves cut into the shapes of apocryphal
animals; drawers flounced down to the ankles, and
flecked with tiny, red roses; stockings clocked with
fêtes galantes, and curious designs; and petticoats
cut like artificial flowers. Some of the women had
put on delightful little moustaches dyed in purples
and bright greens, twisted and waxed with absolute
skill; and some wore great white beards, after
the manner of Saint Wilgeforte. Then Dorat had
painted extraordinary grotesques and vignettes over
their bodies, here and there. Upon a cheek, an old
man scratching his horned head; upon a forehead,
an old woman teased by an impudent amour; upon
a shoulder, an amorous singerie; round a breast, a
circlet of satyrs; about a wrist, a wreath of pale,
unconscious babes; upon an elbow a bouquet of
spring flowers; across a back, some surprising scenes
of adventure; at the corners of a mouth, tiny, red
spots; and upon a neck, a flight of birds, a caged
parrot, a branch of fruit, a butterfly, a spider, a
drunken dwarf, or, simply, some initials. But most
wonderful of all were the black silhouettes painted
upon the legs, and which showed through a white
silk stocking like a sumptuous bruise.

The supper provided by the ingenious Rambouillet was quite beyond parallel. Never had he
created a more exquisite menu. The *consommé
impromptu* alone would have been sufficient to
establish the immortal reputation of any chef.
What, then, can I say of the *Dorade bouillie sauce
maréchale,* the *ragoût aux langues de carpes,* the

ramereaux à la charnière, the *ciboulette de gibier à l'espagnole,* the *pâté de cuisses d'oie aux pois de Monsalvie,* the *queues d'agneau au clair de lune,* the *artichauts à la grecque,* the *charlotte de pommes à la Lucy Waters,* the *bombes à la marée,* and the *glaces aux rayons d'or?* A veritable tour de cuisine that surpassed even the famous little suppers given by the Marquis de Réchale at Passy, and which the Abbé Mirliton pronounced "impeccable, and too good to be eaten."

Ah! Pierre Antoine Berquin de Rambouillet; you are worthy of your divine mistress!

Mere hunger quickly gave place to those finer instincts of the pure gourmet, and the strange wines, cooled in buckets of snow, unloosed all the décolleté spirits of astonishing conversation and atrocious laughter.

Chapter IV

HOW THE COURT OF VENUS BEHAVED
STRANGELY AT HER SUPPER

As the courses advanced, the conversation grew bustling and more personal. Pulex and Cyril, and Marisca and Cathelin, opened a fire of raillery. The infidelities of Cerise, the difficulties of Brancas, Sarmean's caprices that morning in the lily garden, Thorillière's declining strength, Astarte's affection for Roseola, Felix's impossible member, Cathelin's passion for Sulpilia's poodle, Sola's passion for herself, the nasty bite that Marisca gave Chloe, the epilatière of Pulex, Cyril's diseases, Butor's illness, Maryx's tiny cemetery, Lesbia's profound fourth letter, and a thousand amatory follies of the day were discussed.

From harsh and shrill and clamant, the voices grew blurred and inarticulate. Bad sentences were helped out by worse gestures, and at one table Scabius expressed himself like the famous old knight in the first part of the *Soldier's Fortune* of Otway. Bassalissa and Lysistrata tried to pronounce each other's names, and became very affectionate in the attempt; and Tala, the tragedian, robed in roomy purple, and wearing plume and buskin, rose to his feet, and, with swaying gestures, began to recite one of his favourite parts. He got no further than the first line, but repeated it again and again, with fresh accents and intonations each time, and was only silenced by the approach of the asparagus that was being served by satyrs dressed in white. Clitor and Sodon had a violent struggle over the beautiful Pella, and nearly upset a chandelier. Sophie became very intimate with an empty champagne bottle, swore it had made her enceinte, and ended by having a mock accouchement on the top of the table; and Belamour pretended to be a dog, and pranced from couch to couch on all fours, biting and barking and licking. Mellefont crept about dropping love philtres into glasses. Juventus and Ruella stripped and put on each other's things, Spelto offered a prize for whoever should come first, and Spelto won it! Tannhäuser, just a little grisé, lay down on the cushions and let Julia do whatever she liked.

I wish I could be allowed to tell you what occurred round table 15, just at this moment. It would amuse you very much, and would give you a capital idea of the habits of Venus' retinue. Indeed, for deplorable reasons, by far the greater part of what was said and done at this supper must remain unrecorded and even unsuggested.

Venus allowed most of the dishes to pass untasted, she was so engaged with the beauty of Tannhäuser. She laid her head many times on his robe, kissing him passionately; and his skin at once firm and yielding, seemed to those exquisite little teeth of hers, the most incomparable pasture. Her upper lip curled and trembled with excitement, showing the gums. Tannhäuser, on his side, was no less devoted. He adored her all over and all the things she had on, and buried his face in the folds and flounces of her linen, and ravished away a score of frills in his excess. He found her exasperating, and crushed her in his arms, and slaked his parched lips at her mouth. He caressed her eyelids softly with his finger tips, and pushed aside the curls from her forehead, and did a thousand gracious things, tuning her body as a violinist tunes his instrument before playing upon it.

Mrs. Marsuple snorted like an old war horse at the sniff of powder, and tickled Tannhäuser and Venus by turns, and slipped her tongue down their throats, and refused to be quiet at all until she had had a mouthful of the Chevalier. Claude, seizing his chance, dived under the table and came up on the other side just under Venus' couch, and before she could say "One!" he was taking his coffee "aux deux colonnes." Clair was furious at his friend's success, and sulked for the rest of the evening.

Chapter V

OF THE BALLET DANCED BY
THE SERVANTS OF VENUS

After the fruits and fresh wines had been brought
in by a troop of woodland creatures, decked with
green leaves and all sorts of spring flowers, the
candles in the orchestra were lit, and in another
moment the musicians bustled into their places.
The wonderful Titurel de Schentefleur was the
chef d'orchestre, and the most insidious of con-
ductors. His baton dived into a phrase and brought
out the most magical and magnificent things, and
seemed rather to play every instrument than to
lead it. He could add grace even to Scarlatti and
a wonder to Beethoven. A delicate, thin, little man
with thick lips and a nez retroussé, with long black
hair and curled moustache, in the manner of
Molière. What were his amatory tastes, no one in
the Venusberg could tell. He generally passed for
a virgin, and Cathos had nicknamed him "The
Solitaire."

Tonight he appeared in a court suit of white silk,
brilliant with decorations. His hair was curled in
resplendent ringlets that trembled like springs at
the merest gesture of his arm, and in his ears
swung the diamonds given him by Venus.

The orchestra was, as usual, in its uniform of red vest and breeches trimmed with gold lace, white stockings and red shoes. Titurel had written a ballet for the evening divertissement, founded upon De Bergerac's comedy of *Les Bacchanales de Sporion*, in which the action and dances were designed by him as well as the music.

I

The curtain rose upon a scene of rare beauty, a remote Arcadian valley, a delicious scrap of Tempe, gracious with cool woods and watered with a little river. It was early morning and the re-arisen sun, like the prince in the *Sleeping Beauty,* woke all the earth with his lips.

In that golden embrace the night dews were caught up and made splendid, the trees were awakened from their obscure dreams, the slumber of the birds was broken, and all the flowers of the valley rejoiced, forgetting their fear of the darkness.

Suddenly to the music of pipe and horn a troop of satryrs stepped out from the recesses of the woods bearing in their hands nuts and green boughs and flowers and roots, and whatsoever the forest yielded, to heap upon the altar of the mysterious Pan that stood in the middle of the stage; and from the hills came down the shepherds and shepherdesses leading their flocks and carrying garlands upon their crooks. Then a rustic priest, white robed and venerable, came slowly across the valley followed by a choir of radiant children. The scene was admirably stage-managed and nothing could have been more varied yet harmonious than this Arcadian group. The service was quaint and simple, but with sufficient ritual to give the *corps de ballet* an opportunity of showing its dainty skill. The dancing of the satyrs was received with huge favour, and when the priest raised his hand in final blessing, the whole troop of worshippers made such an intricate and elegant exit, that it was generally agreed that Titurel had never before shown so fine an invention.

Scarcely had the stage been empty for a moment, when Sporion entered, followed by a brilliant rout of dandies and smart women. Sporion was a tall, slim, depraved young man with a slight stoop, a troubled walk, an oval impassible face with its olive skin drawn tightly over the bone, strong, scarlet lips, long Japanese eyes, and a great gilt toupet. Round his shoulders hung a high-collared satin cape of salmon pink with long black ribands untied and floating about his body. His coat of sea-green spotted muslin was caught in at the waist by a scarlet sash with scalloped edges and frilled out over the hips for about six inches. His trousers, loose and wrinkled, reached to the end of the calf, and were brocaded down the sides and ruched magnificently at the ankles. The stockings were of white kid with stalls for the toes, and had delicate red sandals strapped over them. But his little hands, peeping out from their frills, seemed quite the most insinuating things, such supple fingers taper-ing to the point with tiny nails stained pink, such unquenchable palms lined and mounted like Lord Fanny's in *Love at all Hazards* and such blue-veined hairless backs! In his left hand he carried a small lace handkerchief broidered with a coronet.

As for his friends and followers, they made the most superb and insolent crowd imaginable, but to catalogue the clothes they had on would require a chapter as long as the famous tenth in Pénillière's *History of Underlinen*. On the whole they looked a very distinguished chorus.

Sporion stepped forward and explained with swift and various gesture that he and his friends were tired of the amusements, wearied with the poor pleasure offered by the civil world, and had invaded the Arcadian valley hoping to experience a new *frisson* in the destruction of some shepherd's or some satyr's *naïveté*, and the infusion of their venom among the dwellers of the woods.

The chorus assented with languid but expressive movements.

Curious and not a little frightened at the arrival of the worldly company, the sylvans began to peep nervously at those subtle souls through the branches of the trees, and one or two fauns and a shepherd or so crept out warily. Sporion and all the ladies and gentlemen made enticing sounds and invited the rustic creatures with all the grace in the world to come and join them. By little batches they came, lured by the strange looks, by the scents and the drugs, and by the brilliant clothes, and some ventured quite near, timorously fingering the delicious textures of the stuffs. Then Sporion and each of his friends took a satyr or a shepherdess or something by the hand and made the preliminary steps of a courtly measure, for which the most admirable combinations had been invented and the most charming music written. The pastoral folk were entirely bewildered when they saw such restrained and graceful movements, and made the most grotesque and futile efforts to imitate them. Dio mio, a pretty sight! A charming effect, too, was obtained by the intermixture of stockinged calf and hairy leg, of rich brocaded bodice and plain blouse, of tortured head-dress and loose untutored locks.

When the dance was ended the servants of Sporion brought on champagne, and with many pirouettes poured it magnificently into slender glasses, and tripped about plying those Arcadian mouths that had never before tasted such a royal drink.

II

'Twas not long before the invaders began to enjoy the first fruits of their expedition, plucking them in the most seductive manner with their smooth fingers, and feasting lip and tongue and tooth, whilst the shepherds and satyrs and shepherdesses fairly gasped under the new joys, for the pleasure they experienced was almost too keen for their simple and untilled natures. Sporion and the rest of the rips and ladies tingled with excitement and frolicked like young lambs in a fresh meadow. Again and again the wine was danced round, and the valley grew as busy as a market day. Attracted by the noise and the merrymaking, all those sweet infants I told you of, skipped suddenly on to the stage, and began clapping their hands and laughing immoderately at the passion and disorder and commotion, and mimicking the nervous staccato movements they saw in their pretty childish way.

In a flash Sporion disentangled himself and sprang to his feet, gesticulating as if he would say, "Ah, the little dears!" "Ah, the rorty little things!" "Ah, the little ducks!" for he was so fond of children. Scarcely had he caught one by the thigh than a quick rush was made by everybody for the succulent limbs; and how they tousled them and mousled them! The children cried out, I can tell you. Of course there were not enough for everybody, so some had to share, and some had simply to go on with what they were doing before.

I must not, by the way, forget to mention the independent attitude taken by six or seven of the party, who sat and stood about with half-closed eyes, inflated nostrils, clenched teeth, and painful, parted lips, behaving like the Duc de Broglie when he watched the amours of the Régent d'Orléans.

Now as Sporion and his friends began to grow tired and exhausted with the new debauch, they cared no longer to take the initiative, but, relaxing every muscle, abandoned themselves to passive joys, yielding utterly to the ardent embraces of the intoxicated satyrs, who waxed fast and furious, and seemed as if they would never come to the end of their strength. Full of the new tricks they had learnt that morning, they played them passionately and roughly, making havoc of the cultured flesh, and tearing the splendid frocks and dresses into ribands. Duchesses and Maréchales, Marquises and Princesses, Dukes and Marshals, Marquesses and Princes, were ravished and stretched and rumpled and crushed beneath the interminable vigour and hairy breasts of the inflamed woodlanders. They bit at the white thighs and nozzled wildly in the crevices. They sat astride the women's chests and consummated frantically with their bosoms; they caught their prey by the hips and held it over their heads, irrumating with prodigious gusto. It was the triumph of the valley.

High up in the heavens the sun had mounted and filled all the air with generous warmth, whilst shadows grew shorter and sharper. Little light-winged papillions flitted across the stage, the bees made music on their flowery way, the birds were gay and kept up a jargoning and refraining, the lambs were bleating upon the hill-side, and the orchestra kept playing, playing the uncanny tunes of Titurel.

The Fruit Bearers

Chapter VI

OF THE AMOROUS ENCOUNTER
WHICH TOOK PLACE
BETWEEN VENUS AND TANNHÄUSER

Venus and Tannhäuser had retired to the exquisite
little boudoir or pavilion Le Con had designed
for the queen on the first terrace, and which commanded the most delicious view of the parks and
gardens. It was a sweet little place, all silk curtains
and soft cushions. There were eight sides to it,
bright with mirrors and candelabra, and rich with
pictured panels, and the ceiling, dome-shaped and
some thirty feet above the head, shone obscurely
with gilt mouldings through the warm haze of
candlelight below. Tiny wax statuettes dressed
theatrically and smiling with plump cheeks, quaint
magots that looked as cruel as foreign gods, gilded
monticules, pale celadon vases, clocks that said
nothing, ivory boxes full of secrets, china figurines
playing whole scenes of plays, and a world of
strange preciousness crowded the curious cabinets
that stood against the walls. On one side of the
room there were six perfect little card tables, with
quite the daintiest and most elegant chairs set
primly round them; so, after all, there may be

some truth in that line of Mr. Theodore Watts—
"I played at picquet with the Queen of Love."

Nothing in the pavilion was more beautiful than
the folding screens painted by De La Pine, with
Claudian landscapes—the sort of things that fairly
make one melt, things one can lie and look at for
hours together, and forget the country can ever
be dull and tiresome. There were four of them,
delicate walls that hem in an amour so cosily, and
make room within room.

The place was scented with huge branches of red
roses, and with a faint amatory perfume breathed
out from the couches and cushions—a perfume
Châteline distilled in secret and called L'Eau
Lavante.

Cosmé's precise curls and artful waves had been
finally disarranged at supper, and strayed ringlets
of the black hair fell loosely over Venus' soft,
delicious, tired, swollen eyelids. Her frail chemise
and dear little drawers were torn and moist, and
clung transparently about her, and all her body was
nervous and responsive. Her closed thighs seemed
like a vast replica of the little bijou she had between them; the beautiful tétons du derrière were
firm as a plump virgin's cheek, and promised a joy
as profound as the mystery of the Rue Vendôme,
and the minor chevelure, just profuse enough,
curled as prettily as the hair upon a cherub's head.

Tannhäuser, pale and speechless with excitement, passed his gem-girt fingers brutally over the
divine limbs, tearing away smock and pantalon
and stocking, and then, stripping himself of his
own few things, fell upon the splendid lady with
a deep-drawn breath!

It is, I know, the custom of all romancers to

paint heroes who can give a lady proof of their valliance at least twenty times a night. Now Tannhäuser had no such Gargantuan felicity, and was rather relieved when, an hour later, Mrs. Marsuple and Doricourt and some others burst drunkenly into the room and claimed Venus for themselves. The pavilion soon filled with a noisy crowd that could scarcely keep its feet. Several of the actors were there, and Lesfesses, who had played Sporion so brilliantly, and was still in his make-up, paid tremendous attention to Tannhäuser. But the Chevalier found him quite uninteresting off the stage, and rose and crossed the room to where Venus and the manicure were seated.

"How tired the poor baby looks," said Mrs. Marsuple. "Shall I put him in his little cot?"

"Well, if he's as sleepy as I am," yawned Venus, "you can't do better."

Mrs. Marsuple lifted her mistress off the pillows, and carried her in her arms in a nice, motherly way.

"Come along, children," said the fat old thing, "come along; it's time you were both in bed."

The Ascension of St. Rose of Lima

Chapter VII

HOW TANNHÄUSER AWAKENED
AND TOOK HIS MORNING ABLUTIONS
IN THE VENUSBERG

It is always delightful to wake up in a new bedroom. The fresh wall-paper, the strange pictures,
the positions of doors and windows, imperfectly
grasped the night before, are revealed with all the
charm of surprise when we open our eyes the
next morning.

It was about eight o'clock when Tannhäuser
awoke, stretched himself deliciously in his great
plumed four-post bed, murmured "What a pretty
room!" and freshened the frilled silk pillows behind him. Through the slim parting of the long
flowered window curtains, he caught a peep of the
sun-lit lawns outside, the silver fountains, the
bright flowers, the gardeners at work, and beneath
the shady trees some early breakfasters, dressed for
a day's hunting in the distant wooded valleys.

"How sweet it all is," exclaimed the Chevalier,
yawning with infinite content. Then he lay back in
his bed, stared at the curious patterned canopy
above him and nursed his waking thoughts.

He thought of the *Romaunt de la Rose,* beautiful, but all too brief.

Of the Claude in Lady Delaware's collection.*

Of a wonderful pair of blonde trousers he would get Madame Belleville to make for him.

Of Saint Rose, the well known Peruvian virgin; how she vowed herself to perpetual virginity when she was four years old†; how she was beloved by Mary, who from the pale fresco in the Church of Saint Dominic, would stretch out her arms to embrace her; how she built a little oratory at the end of the garden and prayed and sang hymns in it till all the beetles, spiders, snails and creeping things came round to listen; how she promised to marry Ferdinand de Flores, and on the bridal morning

---

* The *chef d'œuvre,* it seems to me, of an adorable and impeccable master, who more than any other landscape-painter puts us out of conceit with our cities, and makes us forget the country can be graceless and dull and tiresome. That he should ever have been compared unfavourably with Turner—the Wiertz of landscape-painting—seems almost incredible. Corot is Claude's only worthy rival, but he does not eclipse or supplant the earlier master. A painting of Corot's is like an exquisite lyric poem, full of love and truth; whilst one of Claude's recalls some noble eclogue glowing with rich concentrated thought.

† "At an age," writes Dubonnet, "when girls are for the most part well confirmed in all the hateful practices of coquetry, and attend with gusto, rather than with distaste, the hideous desires and terrible satisfactions of men."
All who would respire the perfumes of Saint Rose's sanctity, and enjoy the story of the adorable intimacy that subsisted between her and Our Lady, should read Mother Ursula's *Ineffable and Miraculous Life of the Flower of Lima,* published shortly after the canonisation of Rose by Pope Clement X in 1671.
"Truly," exclaims the famous nun, "to chronicle the girlhood of this holy virgin makes as delicate a task as to trace the forms of some slim, sensitive plant, whose lightness, sweetness, and simplicity defy and trouble the most cunning pencil." Mother Ursula certainly acquits herself of the task with wonderful delicacy and taste. A cheap reprint of the biography has lately been brought out by Chaillot and Son.

perfumed herself and painted her lips, and put on her wedding frock, and decked her hair with roses, and went up to a little hill not far without the walls of Lima; how she knelt there some moments calling tenderly upon Our Lady's name, and how Saint Mary descended and kissed Rose upon the forehead and carried her swiftly into heaven.

He thought of the splendid opening of Racine's *Britannicus.*

Of a strange pamphlet he had found in Venus' library, called *A Plea for the Domestication of the Unicorn.*

Of the *Bacchanals of Sporion.*

Of love, and of a hundred other things.

Then his half-closed eyes wandered among the prints that hung upon the rose-striped walls. Within the delicate curved frames lived the corrupt and gracious creatures of Dorat and his school, slender children in masque and domino smiling horribly, exquisite lechers leaning over the shoulders of smooth doll-like girls and doing nothing in particular, terrible little Pierrots posing as lady lovers and pointing at something outside the picture, and unearthly fops and huge birdlike women mingling in some rococo room, lighted mysteriously by the flicker of a dying fire that throws great shadows upon wall and ceiling. One of the prints showing how an old marquis practised the five-finger exercise, while in front of him his mistress offered her warm fesses to a panting poodle, made the Chevalier stroke himself a little.

Tannhäuser had taken some books to bed with him. One was the witty, extravagant *Tuesday and Josephine,* another was the score of *The Rheingold.* Making a pulpit of his knees he propped up the opera before him and turned over the pages with a loving hand, and found it delicious to attack Wagner's brilliant comedy with the cool head of the morning.* Once more he was ravished with the beauty and wit of the opening scene; the mystery of its prelude that seems to come up from the very mud of the Rhine, and to be as ancient, the abominable primitive wantonness of the music that follows the talk and movements of the Rhine-maidens, the black, hateful sounds in Alberich's love-making, and the flowing melody of the river of legends.

But it was the third tableau that he applauded most that morning, the scene where Loge, like some flamboyant primeval Scapin, practises his cunning upon Alberich. The feverish insistent ringing of the hammers at the forge, the dry staccato restlessness of Mime, the ceaseless coming and going of the troup of Nibelungs, drawn hither and thither like a flock of terror-stricken and infernal sheep, Alberich's savage activity and metamorphoses, and Loge's rapid, flaming, tonguelike movements, make the tableau the least reposeful, most troubled and confusing thing in the whole range of opera. How the Chevalier rejoiced in the extravagant monstrous poetry, the heated melodrama, and splendid agitation of it all!

At eleven o'clock Tannhäuser got up and slipped off his dainty night-dress, and postured elegantly before a long mirror, making much of himself.

---

* It is a thousand pities that concerts should only be given either in the afternoon, when you are torpid, or in the evening, when you are nervous. Surely you should assist at fine music as you assist at the Mass—before noon—when your brain and heart are not too troubled and tired with the secular influences of the growing day.

Now he would bend forward, now lie upon the floor, now stand upright, and now rest upon one leg and let the other hang loosely till he looked as if he might have been drawn by some early Italian master. Anon he would lie upon the floor with his back to the glass, and glance amorously over his shoulder. Then with a white silk sash he draped himself in a hundred charming ways. So engrossed was he with his mirrored shape that he had not noticed the entrance of a troop of serving boys, who stood admiringly but respectfully at a distance, ready to receive his waking orders. As soon as the Chevalier observed them he smiled sweetly, and bade them prepare his bath.

The bathroom was the largest and perhaps the most beautiful apartment in his splendid suite. The well-known engraving by Lorette that forms the frontispiece to Millevoye's *Architecture du* xviiiᵉ *siècle* will give you a better idea than any words of mine of the construction and decoration of the room. Only in Lorette's engraving the bath sunk into the middle of the floor is a little too small.

Tannhäuser stood for a moment like Narcissus gazing at his reflection in the still scented water, and then just ruffling its smooth surface with one foot, stepped elegantly into the cool basin and swam round it twice very gracefully.

"Won't you join me?" he said, turning to those beautiful boys who stood ready with warm towels and perfume. In a moment they were free of their light morning dress, and jumped into the water and joined hands, and surrounded the Chevalier with a laughing chain.

"Splash me a little," he cried, and the boys teased him with water and quite excited him. He chased the prettiest of them and bit his fesses, and kissed him upon the perineum till the dear fellow banded like a carmelite, and its little bald top-knot looked like a great pink pearl under the water. As the boy seemed anxious to take up the active attitude, Tannhäuser graciously descended to the passive—a generous trait that won him the complete affections of his valets de bain, or pretty fish, as he liked to call them, because they loved to swim between his legs.

However, it is not so much at the very bath itself as in the drying and delicious frictions that a bather finds his chiefest joys, and Venus had appointed her most tried attendants to wait upon Tannhäuser. He was more than satisfied with their skill, and the delicate attention they paid his loving parts aroused feelings within him almost amounting to gratitude, and when the rites were ended any touch of home-sickness he might have felt was utterly dispelled. After he had rested a little, and sipped his chocolate, he wandered into the dressing-room. Daucourt, his valet de chambre, Chenille, the perruquier and barber, and two charming young dressers, were awaiting him and ready with suggestions for the morning toilet. The shaving over, Daucourt commanded his underlings to step forward with the suite of suits from which he proposed Tannhäuser should make a choice. The final selection was a happy one. A dear little coat of pigeon rose silk that hung loosely about his hips, and showed off the jut of his behind to perfection; trousers of black lace in flounces, falling—almost like a petticoat—as far as the knee; and a delicate chemise of white muslin, spangled with gold and profusely pleated.

The two dressers, under Daucourt's direction, did their work superbly, beautifully, leisurely, with an exquisite deference for the nude, and a really sensitive appreciation of the Chevalier's scrumptious torso.

The Third Tableau of Das Rheingold

Chapter VIII

OF THE ECSTASY OF ADOLPHE,
AND THE REMARKABLE
MANIFESTATION THEREOF

As pleased as Lord Foppington with his appearance, the Chevalier tripped off to bid good-morning to Venus. He found her in a sweet muslin frock, wandering upon the lawn, and plucking flowers to deck her breakfast table. He kissed her lightly upon the neck.

"I'm just going to feed Adolphe," she said, pointing to a little reticule of buns that hung from her arm. Adolphe was her pet unicorn. "He is such a dear," she continued; "milk white all over excepting his nose, mouth, nostrils and John. *This* way." The unicorn had a very pretty palace of its own, made of green foliage and golden bars, a fitting home for such a delicate and dainty beast. Ah, it was a splendid thing to watch the white creature roaming in its artful cage, proud and beautiful, knowing no mate, and coming to no hand except the Queen's itself. As Tannhäuser and Venus approached; Adolphe began prancing and curveting, pawing the soft turf with his ivory hoofs and flaunting his tail like a gonfalon. Venus raised the latch and entered.

"You mustn't come in with me, Adolphe is so jealous," she said, turning to the Chevalier, who was following her, "but you can stand outside and look on; Adolphe likes an audience." Then in her delicious fingers she broke the spicy buns and with affectionate niceness breakfasted her snowy pet. When the last crumbs had been scattered, Venus brushed her hands together and pretended to leave the cage without taking any further notice of Adolphe. Every morning she went through this piece of play, and every morning the amorous unicorn was cheated into a distressing agony lest that day should have proved the last of Venus' love. Not for long, though, would she leave him in that doubtful, piteous state, but running back passionately to where he stood, made adorable amends for her unkindness.

Poor Adolphe! How happy he was, touching the Queen's breasts with his quick tongue-tip. I have no doubt that the keener scent of animals must make women much more attractive to them than to men; for the gorgeous odour that but faintly fills our nostrils must be revealed to the brute creation in divine fullness. Anyhow, Adolphe sniffed as never a man did around the skirts of Venus. After the first charming interchange of affectionate delicacies was over, the unicorn lay down upon his side, and, closing his eyes, beat his stomach wildly with the mark of manhood.

Venus caught that stunning member in her hands and laid her cheek along it; but few touches were wanted to consummate the creature's pleasure. The Queen bared her left arm to the elbow, and

with the soft underneath of it made amazing movements upon the tightly-strung instrument. When
the melody began to flow, the unicorn offered up
an astonishing vocal accompaniment. Tannhäuser
was amused to learn that the etiquette of the Venusberg compelled everybody to await the outburst
of these venereal sounds before they could sit
down to déjeuner.

Adolphe had been quite profuse that morning.

Venus knelt where it had fallen, and lapped her
little apéritif.

Chapter IX

HOW VENUS AND TANNHÄUSER
BREAKFASTED AND THEN
DROVE THROUGH
THE PALACE GARDENS

The breakfasters were scattered over the gardens
in tête-à-têtes and tiny parties. Venus and Tannhäuser sat together upon the lawn that lay in front
of the Casino, and made havoc of a ravishing
déjeuner. The Chevalier was feeling very happy.
Everything around him seemed so white and light
and matinal; the floating frocks of the ladies, the
scarce-robed boys and satyrs stepping hither and
thither elegantly, with meats and wines and fruits;
the damask tablecloths, the delicate talk and laughter that rose everywhere; the flowers' colour and
the flowers' scent; the shady trees, the wind's cool
voice, and the sky above that was as fresh and
pastoral as a perfect sixth. And Venus looked so
beautiful.

"You're such a dear!" murmured Tannhäuser,
holding her hand.

At the further end of the lawn, and a little
hidden by a rose-tree, a young man was breakfast-
ing alone. He toyed nervously with his food now

and then, but for the most part leant back in his chair with unemployed hands, and gazed stupidly at Venus.

"That's Felix," said the Goddess, in answer to an enquiry from the Chevalier; and she went on to explain his attitude. Felix always attended Venus upon her little latrinal excursions, holding her, serving her, and making much of all she did. To undo her things, lift her skirts, to wait and watch the coming, to dip a lip or finger in the royal output, to stain himself deliciously with it, to lie beneath her as the favours fell, to carry off the crumpled, crotted paper—these were the pleasures of that young man's life.

Truly there never was a queen so beloved by her subjects as Venus. Everything she wore had its lover. Heavens! how her handkerchiefs were filched, her stockings stolen! Daily, what intrigues, what countless ruses to possess her merest frippery? Every scrap of her body was adored. Never, for Savaral, could her ear yield sufficient wax! Never, for Pradon, could she spit prodigally enough! And Saphius found a month an intolerable time.

After breakfast was over, and Felix's fears lest Tannhäuser should have robbed him of his capricious rights had been dispelled, Venus invited the Chevalier to take a more extensive view of the gardens, parks, pavilions, and ornamental waters. The carriage was ordered. It was a delicate, shell-like affair, with billowy cushions and a light canopy, and was drawn by ten satyrs, dressed as finely as the coachmen of the Empress Pauline the First.

The drive proved interesting and various, and Tannhäuser was quite delighted with almost everything he saw.

And who is not pleased when on either side of him rich lawns are spread with lovely frocks and white limbs—and upon flower-beds the dearest ladies are implicated in a glory of underclothing —when he can see in the deep cool shadow of the trees warm boys entwined, here at the base, there at the branch—when in the fountain's wave Love holds his court, and the insistent water burrows in every delicious crease and crevice?

A pretty sight, too, was little Rosalie, perched like a postilion upon the painted phallus god of all gardens. Her eyes were closed and she was smiling as the carriage passed. Round her neck and slender girlish shoulders there was a cloud of complex dress, over which bulged her wig-like flaxen tresses. Her legs and feet were bare, and the toes twisted in an amorous style. At the foot of the statue lay her shoes and stockings and a few other things.

Tannhäuser was singularly moved at this spectacle, and rose out of all proportion. Venus slipped the fingers of comfort under the lace flounces of his trousers, saying, "Is it all mine? Is it all mine?" and doing fascinating things. In the end, the carriage was only prevented from being overturned by the happy intervention of Mrs. Marsuple, who stepped out from somewhere or other just in time to preserve its balance.

How the old lady's eye glistened as Tannhäuser withdrew his panting blade! In her sincere admiration for fine things, she quite forgot and forgave the shock she had received from the falling of the gay equipage. Venus and Tannhäuser were profuse with apology and thanks, and quite a crowd of loving courtiers gathered round, consoling and congratulating in a breath.

The Chevalier vowed he would never go in the carriage again, and was really quite upset about it. However, after he had had a little support from the smelling-salts, he recovered his self-possession, and consented to drive on further.

The landscape grew rather mysterious. The park, no longer troubled and adorned with figures, was full of grey echoes and mysterious sounds; the leaves whispered a little sadly, and there was a grotto that murmured like a voice haunting the silence of a deserted oracle. Tannhäuser became a little triste. In the distance, through the trees, gleamed a still argent lake—a reticent, romantic water that must have held the subtlest fish that ever were. Around its marge the trees and flags and fleurs de luce were unbreakably asleep.

The Chevalier fell into a strange mood, as he looked at the lake. It seemed to him that the thing would speak, reveal some curious secret, say some beautiful word, if he should dare wrinkle its pale face with a pebble.

"I should be frightened to do that, though," he said to himself. Then he wondered what might be upon the other side; other gardens, other gods? A thousand drowsy fancies passed through his brain. Sometimes the lake took fantastic shapes, or grew to twenty times its size, or shrunk into a miniature of itself, without ever once losing its unruffled calm, its deathly reserve. When the water increased, the Chevalier was very frightened, for he thought how huge the frogs must have become. He thought of their big eyes and monstrous wet feet, but when the water lessened, he laughed to himself, whilst thinking how tiny the frogs must have grown. He thought of their legs that must

look thinner than spiders', and of their dwindled
croaking that never could be heard. Perhaps the
lake was only painted, after all. He had seen things
like it at the theatre. Anyway, it was a wonderful
lake, a beautiful lake, and he would love to bathe
in it, but he was sure he would be drowned if he
did.

Chapter X

OF THE STABAT MATER,
SPIRIDION AND DE LA PINE

When he woke up from his day-dreams, he noticed that the carriage was on its way back to the palace. They stopped at the Casino first, and stepped out to join the players at petits chevaux. Tannhäuser preferred to watch the game rather than play himself, and stood behind Venus, who slipped into a vacant chair and cast gold pieces upon lucky numbers. The first thing that Tannhäuser noticed was the grace and charm, the gaiety and beauty of the croupiers. They were quite adorable even when they raked in one's little losings. Dressed in black silk, and wearing white kid gloves, loose yellow wigs and feathered toques, with faces oval and young, bodies lithe and quick, voices silvery and affectionate, they made amends for all the hateful arrogance, disgusting aplomb, and shameful ugliness of the rest of their kind.

The dear fellow who proclaimed the winner was really quite delightful. He took a passionate interest in the horses, and had licked all the paint off their petits couillons!

You will ask me no doubt, "Is that all he did?"

I will answer, "Not quite," as the merest glance at their jolis derrières would prove.

In the afternoon light that came through the great silken-blinded windows of the Casino, all the gilded decorations, all the chandeliers, the mirrors, the polished floor, the painted ceiling, the horses galloping round their green meadow, the fat rouleaux of gold and silver, the ivory rakes, the fanned and strange-frocked crowd of dandy gamesters looked magnificently rich and warm. Tea was being served. It was so pretty to see some plush little lady sipping nervously, and keeping her eyes over the cup's edge intently upon the slackening horses. The more indifferent left the tables and took their tea in parties here and there.

Tannhäuser found a great deal to amuse him at the Casino. Ponchon was the manager, and a person of extraordinary invention. Never a day but he was ready for a new show—a novel attraction. A glance through the old Casino programmes would give you a very considerable idea of his talent. What countless ballets, comedies, comedy-ballets, concerts, masques, charades, proverbs, pantomimes, tableaux magiques, and peep-shows eccentriques; what troupes of marionettes, what burlesques!

Ponchon had an astonishing flair for new talent, and many of the principal comedians and singers at the Queen's Theatre and Opera House had made their first appearance and reputation at the Casino.

This afternoon the pièce de résistance was a performance of Rossini's *Stabat Mater*, an adorable masterpiece. It was given in the beautiful Salle des Printemps Parfumés. Ah! what a stunning rendering of the delicious démodée pièce de décadence. There is a subtle quality about the music, like the unhealthy bloom upon wax fruit, that both orchestra and singer contrived to emphasise with consummate delicacy.

The Virgin was sung by Spiridion, that soft, incomparable alto. A miraculous virgin, too, he made of her. To begin with, he dressed the rôle most effectively. His plump legs up to the feminine hips of him were in very white stockings clocked with a false pink. He wore brown kid boots, buttoned to mid-calf, and his whorish thighs had thin scarlet garters round them. His jacket was cut like a jockey's, only the sleeves ended in manifold frills, and round the neck, and just upon the shoulders there was a black cape. His hair, dyed green, was curled into ringlets, such as the smooth Madonnas of Morales are made lovely with, and fell over his high egg-shaped creamy forehead, and about his ears and cheeks and back.

The alto's face was fearful and wonderful—a dream face. The eyes were full and black, with puffy blue-rimmed hemispheres beneath them, the cheeks, inclining to fatness, were powdered and dimpled, the mouth was purple and curved painfully, the chin tiny, and exquisitely modelled, the expression cruel and womanish. Heavens! how splendid he looked and sounded.

An exquisite piece of phrasing was accompanied with some curly gesture of the hand, some delightful undulation of the stomach, some nervous movement of the thigh, or glorious rising of the bosom.

The performance provoked enthusiasm—thunders of applause. Claude and Clair pelted the thing with roses, and carried him off in triumph to the tables. His costume was declared ravishing. The men almost pulled him to bits, and mouthed at his great quivering bottom! The little horses were quite forgotten for the moment.

Sup, the penetrating, burst through his silk fleshings, and thrust in bravely up to the hilt, whilst the alto's legs were feasted upon by Pudex, Cyril, Anquetin, and some others. Ballice, Corvo, Quadra, Senillé, Mellefont, Théodore Le Vit, and Matta, all of the egoistic cult, stood and crouched round, saturating the lovers with warm douches.

Later in the afternoon, Venus and Tannhäuser paid a little visit to De La Pine's studio, as the Chevalier was very anxious to have his portrait painted. De La Pine's glory as a painter was hugely increased by his reputation as a fouteur, for ladies that had pleasant memories of him looked with a biased eye upon his fêtes galantes merveilleuses, portraits and folies bergères.

Yes, he was a bawdy creature, and his workshop a regular brothel. However, his great talent stood in no need of such meretricious and phallic support, and he was every whit as strong and facile with his brush as with his tool.

When Venus and the Chevalier entered his studio, he was standing amid a group of friends and connoisseurs who were liking his latest picture. It was a small canvas, one of his delightful morning pieces. Upon an Italian balcony stood a lady in a white frock, reading a letter. She wore brown stockings, straw-coloured petticoats, white shoes and a Leghorn hat. Her hair was red and in a chignon. At her feet lay a tiny Japanese dog, painted from the Queen's favourite "Fanny," and upon the balustrade stood an open empty bird cage. The back-ground was a stretch of Gallic country, clusters of trees cresting the ridges of low hills, a bit of river, a château, and the morning sky.

De La Pine hastened to kiss the moist and scented hand of Venus. Tannhäuser bowed profoundly and begged to have some pictures shown him. The gracious painter took him round his studio.

Cosmé was one of the party, for De La Pine just then was painting his portrait, by the way, which promised to be a veritable chef d'œuvre. Cosmé was loved and admired by everybody. To begin with, he was pastmaster in his art, that fine, relevant art of coiffing; then he was really modest and obliging, and was only seen and heard when he was wanted. He was useful; he was decorative in his white apron, black mask and silver suit; he was discreet.

The painter was giving Venus and Tannhäuser a little dinner that evening, and he insisted on Cosmé joining them. The barber vowed he would be de trop, and required a world of pressing before he would accept the invitation. Venus added her voice, and he consented.

Ah! what a delightful little partie carrée it turned out. The painter was in purple and full dress, all tassels and grand folds. His hair magnificently curled, his heavy eyelids painted, his gestures large and romantic, he reminded one a little of Maurel playing Wolfram in the second act of the Opera of Wagner.

Venus was in a ravishing toilet and confection of Camille's, and looked like K—. Tannhäuser was dressed as a woman and looked like a Goddess. Cosmé sparkled with gold, bristled with ruffs, glittered with bright buttons, was painted, powdered, gorgeously bewigged, and looked like a marquis in a comic opera.

The salle à manger at De La Pine's was quite the prettiest that ever was. The walls, covered with pale blue satin, held in silver panels pictures of shepherds and shepherdesses, of nymphs and heroes, moving in measure in Sicilian landscapes or upon the azure shores of Aegean waters. From the ceiling beautiful divinities made as to throw garlands on the guests, with such effect that one was surprised that the roses, as if unwilling to quit Olympus, would not descend on earth. The floor was covered with a thick-piled carpet, as blue as the Mediterranean at midnight; over it the lackeys and servers moved without a sound in their white satin knee-breeches and sky-blue cutaways laced with silver, and wigs of white spun silk.

De La Pine's butler was a work of art in himself; his great, scarlet, pimply face strangled in a lawn stock, a snowy shirt-frill bulging over his black satin waistcoat, the golden chain of his office depending from his shoulders almost to his knees, he officiated at the beaufet like a virtuoso, pcpping the corks from the bottles, gliding from guest to guest, filling and re-filling the tall glasses, all the while directing the smooth sequence of the dishes with the twitch of an eyelid or the discreet flirt of his napkin. The exquisite wines seemed to acquire a subtler bouquet from his loving gestures, and the plat couvert, or surprise dish, to emit a more ravishing zest from the aweful empressement with which he lifted its cover.

Everyone was in fine form. De La Pine had histoires piquantes which threw them into fits of laughter; Cosmé asked curious riddles and conun-

drums, smiling slyly. The banter grew warm and
intimate, and the painter, in deference to Tannhäuser's travesty, flirted with him outrageously,
saying things to him behind his hand and even
pressing his foot beneath the table. Venus pretended to be jealous, and admonished the Chevalier
with mock severity. Cosmé joined in the fun, and
whispered to Venus that birch discipline might be
in order! At this, Tannhäuser blushed with excitement, for the idea of an amorous fessée always sent
little chills of pleasure and apprehension down his
back. The redundant wine was danced around and
around, and dish succeeded dish. "How sensible
we all are," thought the Chevalier as he gave his
eyes to Venus, pressing his jewelled hand to the
frills that just concealed the swell of his bosom.

They took coffee outside upon the terrace. Here,
a chaste little new moon, precise and delicate as the
luminous paring of a fingernail, hung above a
horizon of suave hills which rolled down to meet
some unimportant faraway darkness that might be
forests. Directly underneath them, seen as from the
Place du Tertre, were the twinkling lights of the
town.

It was a delicious night, warm and windless; the
kind of night, thought the Chevalier as he sipped
his scented liqueur, that invited one to adventures.
And he lost himself in a rêverie of steep streets
and enigmatic doors, secret cellars and walled
gardens, and little bals and dancings where in a
rosy light the lissom couples obey the sobs and
gurglings of an accordeon. How exciting, to wander
through a strange city at night, gathering a nosegay
of its sights and sounds, going ever deeper and
deeper into tiny lanes and alleys that seem to go

nowhere and lead at last to the still waters of a canal, where there are benches and amusing nautical types who are idle and a little lonely. He thought of these things, and of the sweet danger from the passions of the voyous who might seize and ravish one, and this gave him a little frisson of delicious alarm; it was nice to think about, but he didn't know if he would really care for such urgent attention. And yet, if there were strong arms nearby, unseen but ready to rescue one at the very *last* moment—And it looked such a dear little city.

Venus was watching him with an indulgent and clairvoyant smile. "I know what," she said. "Let's go slumming!"

De La Pine and Cosmé seconded her immediately. Tannhäuser pressed her hand.

Chapter XI

OF THE PLEASURES OF THE TOWN

From De La Pine's wardrobe they supplied themselves with cloaks and masks for their nocturnal
revel; the sedan-chairs appeared, borne by some
sturdy fellows in the painter's service, and they
set out, Venus and Tannhäuser in one equipage
and Cosmé and their host in the other. Before
and behind them walked two other of the gilt
valets, bearing torches. A gallant cortège it must
have seemed.

The Chevalier, now tremulous and expectant
as a girl going to her first ball, begged Venus to
take good care of him, and indeed he was in such
a flutter that she had to take him upon her knees,
and kiss him and make much of him before he
recovered himself; even then, he was only completely restored when she opened the empiecement
of her robe and allowed him to take an infantile
liberty. So they passed down the hill and through
some classic gates, across a deserted rondpoint
fringed with a Palladian colonnade and centred
by a slim pillar, and after winding through a few
tortuous streets they came all at once into a little
square all lit up like a birthday party.

It was rather hard to make out the buildings
round about, but it was very like the Place Pigalle,

except that here, instead of the great vulgar brassy café on the south-west corner, there was a venerable church.

No sooner had Venus and Tannhäuser alighted than they were the centre of a small crowd of handsome youths, who proffered their services for whatever game the ladies in fiocchi had a mind to. One vaunted his vigour, another his endurance, still another his genital proportion, whilst one of them whispered in the Chevalier's ear that if Madame was for the pleasures of the little goose, there was none better qualified than himself, at the same time parting his lips and making quaint illustrative movements with his tongue. Their assistance was speedily dispersed by the arrival of De La Pine and Cosmé. The former, unclasping his short cloak, shook his great tasselled codpiece at the youths with an air at once of such threatening and bonhomie that the raff of garçons de joie scattered with little shrieks of fright and laughter; Cosmé sent a handful of silver pieces after them.

The sedan-chairs were dismissed, and the party proceeded afoot to the Café de la Rose. There, they stopped to refresh themselves with some fabulous ices and to listen to the orchestra playing airs from Poupart's *L'Ours qui Danse,* that splendid music where the genius of the people is expressed in valses and polkas whose melodies no one can distinguish or remember, so insistent is the beat, so overlaid are they by trills, appogiaturas, gracenotes and gurgles. The sky above the terrasse, hovering just beyond the brilliance of the lamps, was as tender as a lake at twilight, and made one think of a number of beautiful unfinished things, little scraps of drawing, fragments of refrains, plucked rosebuds, children's love-affairs, and so forth. Had Tannhäuser been in a mood for sentiment, he would have been glad to stay longer. But this evening he merely wished to be amused, and was pleased when they set out down the belanterned boulevard, he himself clinging to Cosmé's arm. After a while he saw they were coming to a street fair.

I am afraid, however, that it would take much too long to describe all the things they saw at the fair and where they went afterwards, before they ended up in the Maison des Raffinés. How Venus and Tannhäuser shared a single horse on the merry-go-round, and what happened in consequence; how the Chevalier won all the prizes at the shooting-gallery, and gave them back again; the remark Venus made to the gentleman who was groping her as they stood in front of the wax-work exhibit of the dangers of the pox, a bon mot so just, witty and to the point that it was on everybody's lips before morning; the extraordinary succession of things that the fortune teller told Tannhäuser, every one of which came true (as those who read this book may find out if they will)— all these matters could furnish material for thrice the space I have allotted them; but I am sure you are more concerned in the progress of our hero's courtship of the goddess, and in how they continued to cement the ties of their liking.

Suffice it to say, therefore, that towards eleven o'clock Tannhäuser had grown just a little bored, and when the Queen suggested they repair to the nearest bagnio he seconded her joyfully. De La Pine said he knew the very place—Mother Hibou's in the rue Ste. Apolline, No. 25, the Maison des

Raffinés. A few minutes later they arrived at the door of this establishment, where the appearance of the painter assured them an immediate welcome. A pretty girl dressed in a pair of long black stockings ushered them into the reception room and went to fetch Madame Hibou.

Venus was idly turning over the albums placed about, in which were pictured a number of quaint groups: the Four Neapolitan Hunchbacks; the Shepherds' Pie; the Lavement Corrective; Snow White and the Seven Dwarfs; and a score of other fantaisies. "Oh dear," she said, with a little moue, "isn't there anything new?"

"Anything you wish, dear lady," said l'Hibou, entering at that minute, "you have only to give it a name." She was a little, grey-faced, dried-up, sharp-eyed, agreeable old thing, dressed in black bombazeen, with square steel spectacles on her nose and grey hair drawn back in a tidy bun; as obliging as an undertaker, as deferential as a head-waiter, and as respectable as you please.

Venus whipped her mask over her face, laughed, and whispered to De La Pine. The painter conferred with the old lady, who nodded several times, smiling primly. "Just so," she said. "A tour of inspection. Ah, and aren't you lucky! There are some fine things going on tonight, let me tell you. This way, my dears, to the panopticon, and mind your step in the dark." She lifted up a piece of tapestry and led them through a little door into a dim passage.

What fun they had as they came to each row of peep-holes! What sights they saw! What frolics and romps! What bagatelles, fredaines and folastreries! For the house was full of roués and rouées, all giving themselves up to their specialties, and enjoying themselves immensely among the wonderful things Mère Hibou had assembled under her roof.

They were especially taken by the scene in a room fitted up like a dainty stable, where a gentleman on all fours, his neck fastened in a stanchion, was impersonating a cow, and was being milked, too! But they were delighted most of all by a young man lying on his back in a little white-walled chamber, his head fitted under a siege on which a charming girl was sitting with a foam of underclothing billowing round her rosy thighs and dimpled derrière—another Anadyomene she seemed!—while a second nymph was palming and persuading his nervous and erect member with gracile fingers. Concerning this young spark, Madame Hibou explained in a whisper that the throne of his divinity was made of clearest glass, and that he was taking his observations sur le vif. And indeed, just at this very moment the watchers received a rare treat, for all at once the seated girl's expression became grave and she bent forwards, making a sign to the other, who infused more vigour into her caresses, so that their endeavours met with a simultaneous success, a double climax instinct with dramatic éclat. Venus clapped her hands softly, and turned a ravished glance on Tannhäuser. "Dear me," said l'Hibou, "that's the fourth time now! Very soon, I shan't have a girl left to sit for him!"

By this time it was growing late. De La Pine inquired what was being played at the little theatre next door.

"Ah," said the old lady, "I was coming to that.

This evening they are presenting something very fine indeed, the famous troupe of Madame Mubouleau, in one of their most celebrated pantomime-operettas. The performance has already begun, and I advise you not to miss the finale! Here is the playbill," and she took a pink paper from her pocket and handed it to the painter who read out:

Madame Mubouleau Presents

PINK CHEEKS
(Les Joues Cramoisies)

with { Mrs. BOWYER!
          and
          Mrs. BARKER!

and the Entire Cast of the Troupe Mubouleau

Two Hours of Fun & Flagellation

Highly Recommended

PINK CHEEKS

"Are you sure it won't be a bore?" Venus asked.

"Upon my word, no," replied the painter. "Bowyer and Barker are real artistes. I can assure you we'll be well entertained."

"Faith, Madam," said Cosmé, with a subtle smile towards the Chevalier, "I believe our fair friend will be enraptured."

"Would you like it, dear?" Venus asked Tannhäuser, slipping her hand under his petticoats, to make sure. "Yes, of course you would, you naughty thing! Not another word."

"Now don't forget to say you were sent by l'Hibou," said the old lady, pocketing a rouleau of gold as they bade her goodnight.

Chapter XII

OF THE OPERETTA

The Théâtre des Deux Mains was a bijou little playhouse which breathed an elegance altogether Regency. Not more than ninety feet by sixty, its proportions were exquisite. The walls were spaced out by panels picturing the gilded shapes of amorous cupidons and caryatides, between which hung portières of dusty-yellow Utrecht velvet embellished with loops, tassels, fleurons and formalised heraldic figures; the ceiling, softly domed and figured with wreaths and curlycues of creamy plaster, was a little low. Everything was arranged in the most intimate way, for the pit had been suppressed altogether, and behind the single row of stalls began the boxes and loges, each able to hold four or five persons.

Although the floor sloped down to a minuscule orchestra-pit, maintaining the classical separation of audience and actors, the stage was so close as to give you the impression of being a part of what was going on; and in fact, when Venus and her party slipped in during the entr'acte, the audience was still deeply moved. The lights were only half up, and everywhere was a buzz of comment and criticism, expressions of appreciation, ejaculations

from behind masks, smiling retorts and suggestive
grimaces. The occupants of some of the boxes had
even drawn the curtains, from behind which came
the sound of slaps and smothered laughter!

Tannhäuser was delighted with everything, especially with the box-openers; for here, instead of
the grumpy old women to whom the playgoer has
become used—though not, I dare say, reconciled—
were a dozen or so beautiful young creatures in
plum-coloured jackets and yellow tapering trousers that strapped under the instep and fitted
smoothly across their behinds; their build, their
delicate features, and the short ringlets that played
around their shoulders left their sex a matter of
doubt; but this ambiguity, De La Pine explained
in a whisper, was matched by their readiness to
sustain the rôle of either.

Then the lights went down, the music began,
and the curtains rose on the second of the two acts,
discovering the interior of an orphanage where a
dozen or more ravishing children, dressed in an
old-fashioned and modest manner, were perform-
ing a graceful gavotte. Circling, dividing, forming
and re-forming in intricate patterns and arabesques, they engrossed the stage with a charming
collective movement, making quaint erotic gestures and accompanying their dance with the sweet
treble of a cheerful little song. Soon the fun became more lively and more risqué, the couples
detaching themselves for a few minutes in the centre of the stage to execute some really naughty pan-
tomime, while the others clapped their hands in
time, beat their little slippers on the floor, and
laughed in a simple, wordless cascade of melody
which was tossed to and fro, from the boys to the

girls and back again, with infinite varieties of expression and cadence.

But all at once there was a roll of drums, the lights on the stage changed to a deep rose, and a drop-curtain swept aside, revealing two statuesque female figures in long white gowns, who had been watching. A wild arpeggio from the harp, like the susurrus of an autumn wind, succeeded, and the chorus of children, wailing, shrank back in a calculated disarray towards the wings; then the matrons advanced slowly, to a solemn, throbbing pizzicato of bass viols.

Their appearance was truly wonderful. With faces painted dead white, mounting false chins and noses which almost met over tiny mouths, their foreheads graced with rows of curls like inverted question marks, and wearing enormous mob-caps which quivered and swayed on their heads, they moved slowly upstage, nodding portentously and making gestures of outrage. A round of applause greeted them, for these were Mrs. Bowyer and Mrs. Barker.

And now the former took a striking attitude, the harp sounded a few notes, and she delivered a glorious recitative, her majestic contralto filling the theatre as she expressed her indignation and horror, her well-nigh disbelief in the testimony of her eyes, while she clasped her hands, raised them in the air and dropped them to her sides, rolling her eyes and shaking her head; an occasional interpolation from Mrs. Barker's argent soprano cut across her words, and then the two voices joined in a sombre and stirring duet in which execrations were mingled with promises of punishment and invocations of the spirit of birch.

The duet ended with three long notes in alt, uttered by the matrons in unison. This was the call to the servants, and as the applause of the audience reached its climax four strapping girls carrying rods rushed on the stage. Now, the orchestra struck up a jolly bourrée, to whose accented rhythm was executed a short and lively bacchanale, the orphans retreating and fleeing, the servant-girls pursuing, grasping and losing; cries of alarm, triumph and vexation mingled with the invigorating music, the dance became a wild rout of flying forms, a whirling kaleidoscope of smock and sash, of bare limb and lacy pantalette, from which at last two of the serving-wenches emerged, each with an orphan securely horsed on her back, and the music ceased with a plangent crash of cymbals.

To the sounds of an exquisite solo by the premier violon, the two captives, a boy and a girl, were now lovingly and ceremoniously untrussed. Ah, what a delightful operation this was! What ravishing contours were exposed, what quiverings, what tremblings and trepidations, what rosy reluctancies, as the plump fesses emerged and the two dear children were prepared for the neat birch rods in the hands of Bowyer and Barker!

Then all was quiet; the tableau arranged itself, each captive flanked by matron and domestic, the remaining children creeping close as at the bidding of fear and fascination, and Mrs. Barker, her rod upraised, began to deliver a thrilling lecture full of the old-fashioned phrases of nursery eloquence. By degrees her emotion mounted, as if like an Homeric hero she were exciting herself by her own threats and vauntings; her voice rose, throbbing and fulminating in sombre crescendi, her

arm gesturing with motions ever more purpose-
ful, until at last, as a superb and stately period
rolled to its close, the twigs descended with a rich
and urgent hiss, and the flagellation commenced
to a softly resumed music.

Tannhäuser, already blushing with pleasure, followed everything eagerly, loving the strokes that
fell so roundly, admiring the art with which the
voices of fesseuse and fessé blended, this one rising, that falling, in a chromatic progression that
decorated in obbligato the gentle but insistent
beat of the bolero whispered by drums and muted
strings. Now, the birch seemed to dominate all the
sounds and movements, as if it, and not the con-
ductor's baton, were leading the music, evoking
the cries of distress and satisfaction, and directing
the reedlike swaying of the chorus from side to
side and the leaps and bounds of the disciplined
urchin. The Chevalier found himself beating time
with the toe of his slipper.

Then the music and cries increased in volume
as flutes and oboes joined in, echoing and mingling
and competing with the singers, and all at once
two other voices added themselves, as Mrs. Bowyer
began to thrash the other culprit; and now the
rhythms multiplied themselves in ingenious coun-
terbeats and syncopations, notes short and long
were exchanged like the repartees of a fugue, and
at last, as agonized trills, roulades and fiorituri
poured from the two children, the stirring quartet
came to an end, its final strains engulfed by roars
and bravos from the audience of deboshed cog-
noscenti.

Fresh melodies and fresh victims succeeded rapidly. The plot became confused, the story lost it-

self, the incidents grew more outrageous, as birch rods were supplanted by thin, lissom canes, these by limber straps, and these in turn by many-tongued martinets. At length, when matters had apparently reached some kind of crisis, there were only the matrons, the four servants, and a beautiful youth, quite nude, occupying the stage. Forming a circle around him, they drove him to and fro between them with the blows of their martinets, laughing silverly, until after a minute or two the boy sank down in an exquisite pose, quite motionless. The lights began to dim, Mrs. Bowyer made a sign with her hand, and in the hush the domestics let down a scale from the proscenium, fastened the youth's wrists to it, and drew him up on tiptoe. The stage was utterly dark for a moment; then a clear rosy light illuminated the three principals, and one saw the two matrons were armed with long, supple whips.

The audience was tense and silent; Tannhäuser himself felt his breath quickening as the blows began to fall. For now make-believe had turned to reality! He reached for the hand of Venus, which squeezed his in moist sympathy, as they both stared at the stage, hearing now the veritable sounds of punishment and the true accents of pain. The youth's body shook, twisted and trembled, his feet danced and kicked, the two whips sang in alternation, and piercing cries filled the little theatre, pleas for mercy, prayers for forgiveness, promises of amendment, all alike met by the matrons' measured replies, calm and judicial, full of ironical sympathy and encouragement, a suave, antiphonal rhetoric made deliciously paradoxical by the steady accompaniment running beneath it, the repeated whistle and report of whipcord on flesh.

"Oddsfish," said Cosmé in a whisper, "'tis artistry with a vengeance, that throws art to the winds." De La Pine nodded, smiling and rubbing his hands.

There was wild applause as the representation came to an end and the fainting youth hung limply in his bonds. Then, as the lights went up and the two Flagellantes advanced to the footlights, hand in hand, bowing, they were greeted by cries of "Unmask, unmask!"—and the next moment, when they twitched off their comic vizards, Tannhäuser saw the two old frights replaced by a pair of handsome, smiling women who at once began to ogle the unattached gentlemen in the side-boxes. Bouquets were thrown from several directions; they were received with bows and courtesies by the divas, who held them to their breasts and then, smiling archly, held up the little notes concealed in them, blowing kisses and flourishing their whips playfully at the admirers they had made.

"If you keep on looking at those creatures that way," Venus smiled at the Chevalier, "I'll be jealous."

Tannhäuser's only response was to draw the curtains of the box violently, to seize the Queen in his arms and press burning kisses upon her neck and shoulders.

"Oh!" she cried after a few moments. "Not here, not here!"

"No," said Mrs. Marsuple, putting her head through the curtains at that instant. "I've engaged the Ducal Suite upstairs. I saw you, my dears, and I knew *just* how you'd be feeling. Come on!"

Chapter XIII

OF THE THIRD ENCOUNTER BETWEEN VENUS AND TANNHÄUSER

Mrs. Marsuple, who insisted on acting as the Chevalier's tirewoman, took him into a beautiful little bathroom, where she undressed him and popped him into a warm, scented bath. Oh, how her cheeks glowed as she feasted upon his limbs, how her eyes sparkled as she laved him all over, and how proud she was of the virility of his mien when she led him to the bed where Venus, in her turn prepared by the discreetly officious Cosmé, was lying in all the splendour of her nudity! Giving little grunts and gasps and chuckles, the good old woman bustled round the amorous pair, smoothing the pillows, straightening the sheets, and in doing so managing to give their bodies little inflaming attouchements.

More than ever, the Chevalier thought what a kind-hearted old thing she was, how devoted to her mistress, how really sweet and charming and thoughtful she was. At last she called Cosmé to come and look at them as they lay with limbs entwined and intervolved, and then, rubbing her hands delightedly, she drew the silk bed curtains and left them to themselves.

Tannhäuser felt as if he were in elysium. Through half-closed eyes he let his gaze glide over the divine form in his arms, while he respired the odours of her hair, her breath and all the secret places of her, from which drifted a subtle perfume that expressed the very essence of love. "O dea certe," he murmured, feeling too happy even to move.

The Queen's eyes met his with an equal languor.

It was so nice, they were both thinking, just to lie like this for a while, like two children who have played a little too hard, and to wait and see what would happen. After all, there was no hurry, and by now they were such good friends that the politeness of any pretence of urgency wasn't necessary. And so they both sank into that sweet rêverie, halfway between slumber and waking, between desire and satiety, which anyone who has experienced it knows is one of the nicest conditions imaginable.

During this time, the Chevalier let his amorous fancy play a dozen pretty tricks. He recalled the eloquence of Mrs. Bowyer, and the graceful and determined play of her whip; he thought of the box-openers at the theatre, of the orphans, of the gentlemen in the side-boxes; observing the Queen's charming back, so smooth and dimpled, he toyed with the idea of a rearward sacrifice to Love. As each of these fantasies passed through his head, he felt an exquisite little quiver pass through him from his head to his heels, but nothing more. Only when he realised that nothing he could think of would put him in a properly loverlike habit, did he become a little put out. "Dear me," he thought, "I must be bewitched."

He saw Venus looking at him with a tender and

indulgent smile, as one of her little hands verified his condition. Stilling his apologies with a kiss, all at once she began to laugh. "Aren't we silly?" she said. "Look, I'm just the same!" And indeed, it was so.

But now he was due for a delicious surprise, in which his admiration for the Queen's ingenuity was only matched by his further sense of the devotion accorded her by her subjects; for calling Mrs. Marsuple and Cosmé, who were playing bezique in the next room, she begged an assistance which was given with such readiness that it was clear they were vastly flattered. In an instant, Tannhäuser saw Venus extended and displaying her treasure to Cosmé, who knelt before it, smacking his lips like a gourmet; and at the same time he found himself turned on his own back by the fat fardeuse who, seating herself comfortably between his thighs, began stroking him with her smooth fleshy palms.

Nothing could have resisted the insinuating skill of her fingers. Not even, I dare affirm, the virtue of that young Saint Gregorovius who in a similar situation, but bound with cords, bit off his tongue in order to preserve his chastity unspotted. The Chevalier was no such prude, and in no time at all his adorable member stood like a stalk of fresh asparagus, which Mrs. Marsuple continued to tease and tickle and fillip and flatter with wonderful sagacity, and when, while occupying one hand in this delightful way, she put the other under his behind and insinuated a suave and active finger, he experienced such glorious sensations that he could have kissed the old trot, then and there.

Instead, he turned his gaze on Venus. Her eyes

were almost closed, and all he could see of them was a thread of white under the dark eyelid, while her lips were parted in a divine smile, and her breath came and went in little zephyrous sighs as Cosmé plied his task. Then, becoming aware of her lover's ardent glance, she opened her eyes and directed at him a swimming look of love. And just then Cosmé signalled to Mrs. Marsuple, who picked the Chevalier up like a baby and laid him gently upon Venus, and guided him into the right way!

But even then the two dear old things didn't forsake their mistress. By now, as you can imagine, they were leaving nothing to chance! And they busied themselves still with their soft palms, Mrs. Marsuple spanking the Chevalier quite smartly, and Cosmé kneading and slapping the warm thighs of Venus, while both of them encouraged the lovers with little cooing cries, smacking their lips, uttering naughty words and playful reproaches, so that matters were settled very soon.

When it was all over, and as the four of them were recruiting themselves with some beautiful pâté-de-foie sandwiches and a bottle of Montrachet, De La Pine came in in a gorgeously flowered dressing-gown, explaining that he had been detained with two of the box-openers. His make-up had suffered terribly, but his spirits not at all, and he gave a droll account of his affair with the two little creatures, in one of whom he protested he had discovered a fellatrice of surpassing artistry, in every way the equal of the celebrated La Boccuccia herself. High praise, this, from a connoisseur like the painter!

They were all very jolly and relaxed. And indeed it would be hard to find another five persons so well suited to enjoy each other's society as these. The party broke up at last in the small hours. Venus and Tannhäuser decided to stay where they were until the following day.

"Good night, my dears, good night. And thank you ever and ever so much, dear Master," said Venus to the painter. "It was a wonderful party, and I had a perfectly lovely time." And turning to Tannhäuser, she curled herself up in his arms and fell asleep immediately.

The others resumed their dominos, and crept out, whispering good-nights. Mrs. Marsuple was the last to retire. Stepping noiselessly round the room, she blew out the candles one by one, and in the faint light of dawn that was beginning to gild the edges of the curtains, she stood for a moment motionless before the sleeping lovers, her fat forefinger held before her lips, before slipping from the chamber.

Chapter XIV

OF HOW THE CHEVALIER TANNHÄUSER
WITHDREW FROM THE HILL OF VENUS

That was the way the days went by at the Court of
Venus. Every afternoon there was some kind of
excursion, and every night some entertainment. For
Tannhäuser, the weeks took on the appearance of
a pattern diversified with the ever-repeated figures
of pic-nic, fête champêtre, concert, comedy, ballet
and ball, the whole decorated by the thousand
and one shapes, antic or graceful, that thronged
the parks and corridors and drives. Sometimes, it
is true, when he felt no inclination for spectacle,
junket or revel, he would spend a delightful evening by himself in the Royal Library, which was
full of rare and curious books and prints and
boasted a variety and completeness second only
to the Ashbee Collection. But most of all he liked
the early mornings, when, after stealing from his
own bed into that of the Queen, he would lie
studying for as much as an hour the beauty of
her sleeping face, and luxuriate in the sentiment
of his affection for her. Without knowing it, you
see, he was really becoming bored.

Then one morning Venus began talking in her
sleep. Tannhäuser listened in spite of himself for

a few moments; for she was reciting a list of names. "Adonis, Anchises, Ares—" she murmured.

The Chevalier stopped his ears. But when he took his polite fingers away a minute later she was still reciting softly her amorous alphabet. "—Ulrich von Lichtenstein, Heinrich von Limburg, Leonard Lipstein—" He blushed, and put his fingers in his ears again. But after a while he became curious to hear his own name.

"Will she pause after speaking it?" he asked himself anxiously. "Will she not pay it at least the tribute of a sigh?" And he sighed himself, watching the beautiful rosy lips forming the syllables with such composure.

"—Taliesin, Tannhäuser, Thomas the Rhymer—"

His own name had been pronounced exactly like the rest.

He sighed still more deeply, and as he did so he heard a muffled laughter coming from behind the great painted screen beside the bed. He jumped out of bed in a fury, to chastise the insolence of the mocker, but discovered it was only Claude and Clair who were lightheartedly buggering each other on the carpet, turn and turn about, without a thought for anything else. For the first time since his arrival under the Hill, the Chevalier's reaction to such a scene was one of distaste.

"Alas!" he thought an instant later, "that I should ever catch myself in a censorious vein! A pox on it, I shall turn prude next."

Gathering his silk night-dress about him, he tiptoed quietly from the Queen's chamber and went back to his own bedroom, dressed himself in the plainest manner possible, and set out for a walk. Soon he had left the ornamental gardens behind, and was thridding the mazes of a gigantic and gloomy wood. Great oaks and beeches cast their shadows all around him, there were ancient willows writhing themselves into the shapes of ancient women, and thick creepers strewed the ground like horrid snakes. It was quite dark now under the trees, and at any other time the Chevalier would have been terribly frightened by the Doré-like landscape; but at present he was a stranger to any emotion save his own melancholy and pique. At last he espied a faint light, that was coming from a little pavilion right in the middle of the darkest part of the forest, and as he was already becoming bored with his morning ramble he went towards it. He went up first of all to a window and looked in, and was at once stricken with dismay.

Against one wall there stood a sturdy, old-fashioned garrote in which a beautiful, nude, pink and white boy was strapped; a bare-armed figure in a hangman's smock and mask was at the wheel, while extended on a chaise-longue, watching the scene, was a young man called Cascabel—a heavy, sullen, good-looking youth whom Tannhäuser had seen occasionally at Court, where he never seemed to be enjoying himself in the slightest. Now, he was wearing nothing but a long, dark, hooded cloak, and between his knees lolled another ravishing boy who was loving him with suave gestures.

As Tannhäuser looked through the window, the wheelsman was easing the cord; but a second later, at a sign from Cascabel, he reversed the movement of his hands. The victim's cheeks swelled, his eyes bulged; while Cascabel, glaring at him with working features, appeared about to come at any moment. But when the boy's tongue popped from his mouth, Tannhäuser, with a cry of indignation, leapt over the window-sill, pulled out his dagger and in a trice had cut the cord around the fair sufferer's neck.

The next moment he was aware of a number of things. Of a soft report from the boy's body; of a hardly suppressed burst of laughter from the executioner; of Cascabel, limp and entirely put out, drawing his cape about him and stamping out of the room in a terrible huff. The Chevalier, looking dazedly at the collapsed rubber toy at his feet, suddenly realised that his bêtise would be all over the Court in no time. Uttering an imprecation, he leapt back through the window and plunged into the shelter of the woods, only too anxious to hide his blushes for his piece of folly and impertinence.

Truly, everything seemed to be going wrong that day!

Slowing into a walk, Tannhäuser engaged in bitter reflections. "Ah, country of Love," he thought, "and you, shapes of a thousand varieties of desire, how plain your folly shows to a mortal! For to what end are all these pranks and pleasures? Out on your venery! When all's done 'tis but a painted motion—a precious fooling rather, like dicing for no stakes."

When he returned to breakfast with Venus he was still mumchance and distrait. In some funny way this fresh, beautiful morning, a twin to the first one he had spent here, now seemed to possess an air of tired, autumnal sadness. In vain did Venus tempt him with some lovely melons.

"My dear Chevalier," she said at last, observing

that for all his silence he directed towards her, ever and anon, a searching and speculative regard, "pardon me, I pray, and believe that it is only the depth of my regard for you that leads me to deface a resolution of seemliness and silence, by making so bold as to inquire the ground of your indisposition."

"Ah," replied Tannhäuser, fetching a sigh, "Your Majesty's concern makes me only too aware of the inexcusable colour of my behaviour—and that, too, in presence of one to whom I am beholden for a thousand flattering attentions, and a thousand acts of grace. But oh, believe not that my sense of your bounties has suffered diminution, any more than have the feelings of gratitude that animate my heart. Had they done so, I were other than myself; and, therefore, the less yours. Nay, Madam, it is the very depth of my sentiment for you which perturbs me, when I bring it into comparison with the dubious strength of a reciprocal attachment which may not well withstand my petition to your grace."

"How now, Chevalier," said the Queen in accents of mild reproach. "Dubious, say you? What marks have I not given of my esteem and partiality? Unless," and here she paused, blushing slightly, "unless it be that your sensibility has been wounded by a seeming indication that my attachment is marked by more warmth than delicacy."

"Not so, adorable creature!" cried Tannhäuser, pressing her hand. Emotion choked him; he could say no more for a moment; and indeed, when he was able to stammer forth his request to the Queen he did so with such halting locutions and syntactical awkwardness as would be quite out of place in the chronicle. But as he continued his imagination took fire, his aplomb returned, his tongue smoothed itself, and he pursued his discourse with something of his usual warmth and eloquence.

"Think, think, my love," he murmured, "of the pretty fingers and fair limbs, of the blue eyes archly dancing and the bright-clustering golden curls! Think, too, of the rapture, the dear domestic bliss, of hearing the lisp and prattle of infant lips and the patter of tiny feet! And be sure, Your Majesty's palace is the only place for such a child to be born and reared, the only place where I could be sure she would not acquire absurd ideas or vulgar prejudices. For it shall be a girl, I warrant you."

But Venus was already looking crestfallen. "Oh dear," she said, "I'm afraid it's out of the question. It isn't allowed here, you know. It's against regulations."

"But regulations," said the Chevalier, assuming his most insinuating leer, "are meant to be broken."

"Oh, I didn't mean it that way. No, it just doesn't work. It's not only *me*, you see; everyone else here is in the same fix. And anyway, I've tried it before."

Tannhäuser was silent for a full minute, his face pale, as he digested this intelligence which put an end to all his ambitions of distinction and even to the resuscitation of his teazed amour propre.

"Well, then," he said, masking his distress with a casual air, "I'd best be off."

Venus turned her beautiful eyes on him interrogatively, but said nothing.

The lovers parted that afternoon beside the ornamental water in the great park. It was all very informal; the Chevalier wished to make a farewell speech to her, but Venus stopped his mouth and kissed him. She looked sad, he thought, but not heartbroken, standing there in the yellow sunlight in her light muslin dress.

"I suppose I shan't be seeing you again," she said.

"Indeed, I do not know," said Tannhäuser gravely. "The future is dark."

She sighed, then took his hand in both of hers and pressed it warmly. "Well, whatever happens, my dear Chevalier, I shall always be here. You will remember that, won't you?"

He hardly saw her. "Farewell, Your Majesty," he said, gazing over her head to the green, suntipped splendour of the trees. "However you think of me in the future, if indeed I may flatter myself you will spare me a thought, I beg you will do so with more kindness than I deserve. No one can be more sensible than I of my folly, nor of your excellent good sense. Only consider, Madam, that I am a mortal, and as such, a feeder on illusions. Your divinity knows nothing of such an appetite; but let your generosity condone what your judgment must disapprove. And so, once again, farewell." He heaved a little sigh, and gestured with his hand. "Be yours to pluck the day, to gather rosebuds in this eternal springtime; be mine to toil onwards through the earth, my face fixed on a receding goal, a pilgrim of the absolute."

He bowed deeply over her hand, then turned and mounted the barouche-landau driven by Curb, the Queen's coachman; a few minutes later he was set down by the gate of the dark corridor giving access to the outer world.

Firmly, he stepped across the threshold and braved the light of reality.

Venus Between Terminal Gods

Chapter XV

OF THE CHEVALIER
TANNHÄUSER'S FORTUNES AT THE
GAMING TABLES, AND HOW HE SOUGHT
ABSOLUTION

It was September now in the upper world, and the paysage was enchanting. As Tannhäuser tripped down the green valley of Marienthal he let his gaze rove around him, approving now the clusters of cottages beneath him, now the mountains clothed in black fir-trees or damp meadows. He took the little field-path that leads to the Gotha road with its intersection of bridges and green rivulets. As he walked along, his eyes fixed on the heights of the Wartburg far in the west, drinking in the scents and sounds of the country, he felt his spirits rising. He began to hum the polka from *La Belle Hélène* of Offenbach.

"There's no doubt of it," he thought, "the people down there are very agreeable, but the atmosphere was—well, just a little stuffy."

He was still in a mood of pleasant elation when he reached Gotha that evening, where he put up at the Inn of the Golden Anchor, his distinguished air and rich dress securing for him the most hand-

some suite of apartments the house boasted. It was
only after a light but delicious dinner that he
bethought him of the condition of his purse, and
opening it, found it contained but a single gold
piece. He smiled at his absent-mindedness, and
decided to take a stroll around the little town and
explore its possibilities for distraction.

It was about the fall of the evening, at that time
when the equilibrium between Day and Night for
some time holds the air in a tender suspension
between an unwillingness to leave the light and
a natural impulse into the realm of darkness, that
the Chevalier sallied forth of his lodging and bent
his steps towards the Koenigstrasse, where he saw
such a prodigious number of torches, that the day,
by help of these auxiliary forces, seemed to con-
tinue its dominion; the owls and bats apprehend-
ing their mistake in counting the hours, must have
retired again to a convenient darkness; for Madam
Night was no more to be seen than to be heard in
this jolly town.

The air was mild, but delightfully fresh and
fragrant; along the crowded Koenigstrasse the
lights blazed and swam from a score of places of
entertainment, and everyone was in holiday mood.
The Chevalier, catching the happy temper of the
crowd, relaxed from the dignity of his rank some-
what, and pleasing himself with the looks of admiration which followed him, mingled boldly with
the throng; the glances of the women he answered
with a caressing smile, ever and anon pausing to
reward some special beauty with the salute of his
fingers.

But word of his identity spread swiftly. Exclama-
tions of "Tannhäuser!" "It is the Chevalier Tann-

häuser!" "The famous, the incomparable Tannhäuser!" began to follow him. His progress was
soon graced with a retinue of whispers, little cries
and amorous murmurs. Then the attentions became more marked; he felt the clasp, first of one
little hand, then of another, and another, on his
silken sleeves; he beheld lovely, beseeching faces
turned on him from all sides; perfumed notes
were thrust into his unwilling hand; and all at
once he was aware of a beautiful arm, bearing aloft
a tiny pair of scissors, stretched towards his flowing curls.

At that instant he saw before him the entrance
of the great gaming saloon, and disengaging himself gently from the adoring mellay he turned and
entered. By now he was quite out of breath, his
spirits were flurried, and he was thankful for the
happy chance that had led him to this place. Here,
he told himself, the attractions of his face and
figure would yield precedence to those of the green
tables of fortune and the shifting piles of gold.

In the saloon a thousand candles flared in their
sconces, and a low hum as of bees rose from the
serried ranks of gamesters who, pallid and intent,
studied the sequences of cards, the faces of dice,
and the caprices of the rolling ball. All at once the
Chevalier himself caught the contagion. Ah, it was
in vain that he sought, for a moment, the distraction of a mirror! Even the sight of himself could
not, for once, absorb him entirely. Shrugging his
shoulders, he leaned over the table of roulette and
cast his gold piece gracefully on the number which
typified all his earthly hopes. A minute later the
ball found the little green stall of that mystic
zero, and Tannhäuser's bright piece, heretofore

his single soldier on the green field of battle, was joined by thirty-six companions from the camp of the enemy. With a smile and a wave of his hand, he bade them stay where they were.

None the less, it was with a certain astonishment that he saw that on the next roll he had won again, and that his stake now amounted to well-nigh fourteen hundred pieces. Intrigued, a little piqued by this abject surrender of fortune, he decided to leave his winnings once again. There was a buzz of admiration from the onlookers, interspersed with an oath or two for his folly. Everyone else had stopped playing. The croupier had turned white; the hands with which he spun the wheel were trembling. Once again the ivory ball was in motion.

The Chevalier, calculating swiftly, made a movement of impatience. "Heavens," he was thinking, "how thoughtless of me! If I win, I cannot possibly carry all the money in the pockets of this dress," when he became aware that the light in the great room had been failing; by now, in fact, all the candles were burning a sickly blue. At the same time, he saw a portly official in black, as bald as an egg, flanked by two creatures in livery, at his side; the wheel was stopped in mid-course, and he heard this person requesting him, in tones of apology and superstitious horror, to play no more, for that the house could enter into no contest with the powers of evil; and as the fellow uttered these words he crossed himself.

Tannhäuser started back in outrage. He raised his slender cane, thinking for an instant to chastise the insolence of this menial; then he saw the movement of withdrawal of everyone from him, he looked again at the flickering candles, and lowered his arm. The man in black, bowed almost to the ground before him, signed with a shaking hand to the two lackeys; in a trice the Chevalier's winnings were swept from the board and bestowed in a pair of leathern bags, and he himself was ushered to the door and the bags thrust into his hands.

In the street, surveying for a moment the closed door of the gaming hell with indescribable feelings, Tannhäuser shook his head slowly; then he returned, musing deeply, to the inn.

The following day saw the restoration of his spirits. The people of the inn displayed a properly respectful, even slavish, demeanour; the news of his débusquement at the casino had either not reached them, or, as was more likely, they were indifferent to anything but their guest's gold. Tannhäuser was pleased by this affirmation of inn-keeperly values, and distributed largesse lavishly before he set forth in the smart chaise and four which he purchased from the landlord. In answer to the postilions' query of whither he wished to go, the Chevalier made a vague but authoritative gesture. "Proceed straight ahead," he murmured, and sank back against the cushions. The whip cracked, the horn was blown, the horses shook their gleaming frontlets, and the chaise moved out of Gotha.

"En route!" exclaimed Tannhäuser to himself, experiencing in anticipation all the ecstasy of Dr. Samuel Johnson himself, at the idea of being whirled over the earth in such a conveyance.

And now the chaise passed through a delicious champaign, diversified by little brooks, woods and bridges, with ever and anon a neat grey castle perched on a green hill against a background like those in Dürer's pictures. The sky was high and blue, the air like perfume; there were still rustics at work in the autumn fields, who looked up, bowing and courtesying in a very proper manner, as the handsome equipage sped by. "A sweet country," thought the Chevalier, and lulled by the motion of the carriage, he sunk at last into a light slumber from which he was awakened when they arrived at twilight in front of a venerable little church in the midst of fields, and heard the gentle chiming of the sacring-bell. "Stop here!" he called to the postilions, and he alighted and entered.

It was dark inside; for Night, as Barbey d'Auré-villy well observes, always falls earlier in churches than it does anywhere else. Two long thin candles on each side of the nave, and the lamp of the sacristy, a fixed star in the gloom of the choir, threw a glimmer rather than a light. After a while, when his eyes were used to the darkness, Tann-häuser gazed around him, seeking the confessional; the next minute he had entered and was kneeling by the grating of the box.

For a moment, facing the priest whom he could barely see, he was not sure how to begin. There was such a lot he had to say! He began to speak. As he did so, the flames of the twin candles in the nave wavered. "Yes, my son, yes," the aged priest was murmuring. "A little louder, if you please. I am a bit deaf, you know. Where did you say you had been? Excuse me, I did not catch—"

"In the Hill of Venus," answered Tannhäuser, trembling as he repeated the fateful words. With terror he saw the candles guttering wildly.

"There is something evil here," muttered the

priest. "*Abi, Sathanas, abi!* God be with me," he added. "What can it be?"

"Father, it is only I," said Tannhäuser, now really alarmed. "A poor sinner seeking absolution. Ah, I have sinned, I have sinned!" And his words came in a torrent.

"Yes, yes. Go on, my son. Yes, yes—No, no! No more, impious and abandoned man, in the name of Heaven!"

The Chevalier drew back in consternation. The old man was shaking his head slowly, like a dog.

"These are grave matters, my son," he went on, in a lower tone, "and quite beyond my jurisdiction. You must understand," he paused and blew his nose, "you must realise that sins like yours are something special. I'm afraid you must go to Rome with them—to the Holy Father himself, in fact. No doubt he can give you absolution. But I wouldn't care to take such a responsibility on myself."

Tannhäuser remained silent, his body bowed, his face in his hands. At last he found his voice. "To Rome, then, I shall go." He paused, and as he rose he spoke with great humility. "Would it be of any effect, father, if I went there barefoot?"

"I doubt it," said the old man in a drier tone. "But of course it can do no harm."

Tannhäuser knelt, and solemnly recorded his vow.

Chapter XVI

OF THE CHEVALIER TANNHÄUSER'S
PILGRIMAGE

That night Tannhäuser was weighed upon by
dreams of unimaginable desolation and ennui.
He found himself at the tiller of a tiny boat
scudding through the mountainous wastes of an
ocean, among huge waves whose foam curled
behind and before him into fantastic faces of
Medusas, sinister old men, maidens drowned in
their hair and heraldic beasts, oppressing him with
an air of menace, fury and appeal; the wind
howled, and at his feet a terrified kitten was mew-
ing, rubbing itself against his legs; with every
wave that broke over the boat, he was in agony
lest the animal be carried away. Holding the main-
sheet in his teeth, he tried with his free hand to
catch the soaked body which continued to evade
him, until he seized it at last by the tail; spitting,
pussy twisted free and fell over the side, her final
scream for help lost in the storm. Then the scene
changed, and he was in a terrible, sunstruck,
ochreous desert, flat as a table, and full of weird
shadows; beside him the kitten was lying, stretched
out in the last extremities of thirst, its eyes glazed,
its tongue lolling. "Dear God," thought the Cheva-

lier, "I must find it drink, the poor thing." He sought to collect some moisture in his own mouth, but his throat was dry as ashes. He put his teeth to his arm, and was rewarded by a gush of blood; but when he proffered the wound to his companion the little tongue extended, bathed itself for an instant in the ruby flood, and then fell stiffly sideways. A wave of horror passed over him. Understanding that he had somehow lost his own immortal soul, he awoke in unspeakable perturbation.

Although it was barely dawn, Tannhäuser rose, dressed himself and gave orders for his chaise to be made ready. "To Rome! To Rome!" he cried to the sleepy postilions. And soon he was being borne southward like the wind. Some time had elapsed before he bethought him of his vow to make his pilgrimage barefoot. When he did so he stopped his equipage, removed his shoes and stockings, and descended, bidding the postilions follow him along the road.

Soon his feet were bleeding from the rough stones. Ah, those tender extremities were not made for such work! Limping, weeping, crying out at the stab of each cruel anfractuosity, he discovered in less than an hour that he could go no further; he sat down at the roadside, his head in his hands, the very picture of despondency. "Ah, Lord, what shall I do?" he cried. "I had as well undertaken to walk to Rome on my hands, like a tumbler." Then a saving thought struck him, and he remounted the chaise. And still barefoot in obedience to his vow, he let himself be carried on his way.

Thus he traversed Germany and France; thus

he crossed the celebrated Alps and descended into
the smiling plain of Lombardy. The face of the
countryside had long since become indifferent to
him; unmoved alike by rural beauty and mountainous splendour, he remained sunk in a gloomy
lethargy, failing to notice even the altered demeanour of his servants who were indeed convinced
they had to do with a madman and had already laid
their plans; so that the Chevalier awoke late one
morning at the inn in Milan to find the scoundrels
had decamped with his chaise and horses, thought-
fully taking with them the remainder of his gold.

The defection had the result of rousing him
from his torpor. He felt his spirits lighten. "It
was undoubtedly a punishment of Providence," he
reflected as he stood in the inn-yard, "for the half-
hearted fulfilment of my vow. One does not cheat
the Almighty. He has signified His displeasure by
stripping me of my conveyance and my gold, but
in that very act may I not discern a tacit accept-
ance, perhaps even an approval, of the penance
which I imposed upon myself and which His in-
struments have obliged me to carry out au pied
de la lettre?" Then he reflected that without money
he would be unable to settle his reckoning at the
inn. At that very moment, indeed, he was aware
of the hôtelier surveying him with an air of
haughtiness and suspicion; and he realised he must
assume the wisdom of the serpent. Without vouch-
safing the fellow any answer to his question touching the removal of his chaise, Tannhäuser entered
the house and bespoke a splendid breakfast.

Afterwards he mounted to his rooms, and calling
for pens and paper, set about drawing up a memo-
randum of his sins, lest any perturbation he might

feel in the presence of His Holiness should cause him to omit, in his laying bare of so much unexampled flagitiousness, certain peccadilloes, quasi-transgressions, minor sodomies, and other things. But he had only exhausted the resources of the fourth sheet of his foolscap, bringing down the chronicle of his misdeeds to his tenth year, when he grew aware of a troubling element in his consciousness and an involuntary turgescence.

"A plague on memory!" he exclaimed.

Indeed, all those pretty tricks of childhood, his precocious attachment to Mademoiselle Fanfreluche the nursery governess, their merry games at bedtime, the delightful caresses which like favourable breezes had urged on the forward season of his youth, all those charming things which had made of him such an early and impassioned connoisseur of naughtiness, had arisen before him clothed in the warm and glowing hues of poetry.

Sighing, he laid down his pen, and sought to recall his wandering thoughts and wayward senses. It was no use. His fancy, just such another wayward child, would sport in the meadows of remembered wrongdoing, weaving a flowery chain of scenes redolent of a thousand delicate indecencies, the quirks and antics of a happy Cherubino; while his flesh, like a partner in the dance, quivered and throbbed in a manner quite unfitting a penitent. His recollections darted forward to his first exploit as a lover, to the act, at once result and retort, which followed on his first birching by his English governess—the summary ravishment of that spinster who, too surprised to resist or cry out, had yielded her guarded treasure with something close to complaisance. He smiled as he recalled her burning cheeks, the downcast eyes behind her steel spectacles, her air of confusion and délice.

"Dear me," he thought. "In what category does that come? Was it a rape or a seduction?" For the first time he was moved to regret that he had not a spiritual director versed in the niceties of such subjects, someone like the good Father Sanchez or the subtle Jesuit Luis Molina, to clear up his difficulties. Then, recovering his sobriety, he resumed his writing.

When he had finished, the manuscript formed a bulky pacquet which he sealed with care and sewed in the lining of his coat. It was now after two o'clock in the morning, and turning to the bed he tore the sheets in strips and fashioned from them a rope which he knotted to the bed's foot, throwing the other end out of the window. Then, commending himself to the protection of Heaven, he launched himself from the sill and began to descend; this was accomplished with safety, only that his strength having given out when he was some six feet from the ground, he concluded his journey in a summary fashion, landing in a heap of compost which had been taken from the stables that very day.

This misadventure caused him to recover all his spirits in a twinkling, so that, while resting where he had fallen for a minute or two, he was ready to laugh heartily at the condition he was now in, being thoroughly bemired from head to foot. A happy thought struck him. Now, at least, did his outer semblance figure forth his inward state! He no longer offered to his own shocked contemplation the contrast between an exterior rich and elegant and a soul steeped in all manner of nastiness. Then he rose and quietly slipped from the inn-yard into the street.

But we simply cannot follow the Chevalier during the intermediary stages of his journey. The beggarly shifts to which he was put, the meanness of his adventures, the deterioration of his splendid clothing, are all matters too *low* to find a place in this record. Accordingly, I resume the history of his pilgrimage with his arrival in the famous city of Rome. By then he was in rags and tatters, his cheeks covered by the plush of a three weeks' beard, he was barefoot and unspeakably dirty. Thanks, however, to this picturesque and interesting appearance, he had not long to wait before securing an audience with the Supreme Pontiff— for the Vatican Cærimonarius and the Papal Chamberlain, impressed by the signs of such unexampled misery, believed they must betoken that eccentric sanctity which commanded more respect in those days than it does at present.

Knowing nothing of this, the Chevalier was full of fear and trembling; and when bidden to enter the Room of Audience, he moved uncertainly and with effort, mainly solicitous of the pacquet which he still clasped to his ragged breast.

Chapter XVII

OF HOW THE CHEVALIER TANNHÄUSER
HAD AUDIENCE OF THE POPE

At the end of the domed and pillared Chamber of Audience, upon the winged and gilded throne on its triple-tiered dais, the Supreme Pontiff was seated. He wore the papal habit of white taffetas with cincture, the rochet of fair linen, and the embroidered stola; on his feet were slippers of ermine and crimson velvet; on his head reposed the pontifical diadem, the famed triregno, a conical cap woven of the plumage of white peacocks, feathered and embroidered like a piece of fancy-work, set with the sapphires of the Lord Paul P.P. II, and encircled with three crowns of gold. His expression was venerable, his glance mild yet piercing, and his whole aspect as majestic as at his coronation itself, when the Cardinal Archdeacon, proffering him the diadem, had solemnly intoned, "Receive this tiara adorned with three crowns, and know Thyself to be the Ruler of the World, the Father of Princes and of Kings, and the Earthly Vicar of Our Saviour."

Still trembling, the ragged, forwandered Tannhäuser knelt down before him and kissed the cross embroidered on the shoe, the crosses on the ends of the stola, and the Ring of the Fisherman on his right forefinger.

"Holy Father," he murmured, "grant me, I beseech thee—me, the most unhappy of thy children—a complaisance for my sins." He could say no more; all his fine words were gone. With a despairing gesture, he proffered his sinful budget to the Apostle.

The voice of the Pontiff was heard. "Be not dismayed, my son," he said. "Mercy is infinite."

The Chevalier dared not raise his eyes. He waited in silence; after what seemed an eternity he stole a glance upwards, and caught his breath. The Holy Father, leafing rapidly through the initial pages of the memorial, was smiling slightly. The Chevalier lowered his eyes swiftly, his whole being quivering with hope. Then he heard an ominous sound. Once more peeping upward, he met a terrible glance which penetrated him like a lightning flash. Slowly, deliberately, His Holiness held up the final pages of the vile record; the sheets fell from his outraged fingers, one by one, to the floor.

"Holy Father," Tannhäuser began. The Pope raised his hand, not in benediction but for silence.

"Chevalier Tannhäuser," he said, "thou are assuredly lost."

The suppliant prostrated himself, his hands joined in mute appeal, his attitude imploring mercy. Above his head the Servant of Servants' voice boomed out:

"Aye, naught can save thee, wretched man! Not fasting, watching, or almsgiving, not flagellation night and day! Starving on bread and water, wearing odious and ugly clothes—"

The Chevalier shrank back.

"—Doing menial service to thy natural inferiors—"

The Chevalier turned pale. The orotund voice rolled on;

"—Wheeling manure in barrows, herding with vulgar men—"

The Chevalier fell, hiding his face in his hands. The intolerable, sonorous voice tolled on:

"Nay, none of these can serve to expiate thy guilt. Not even a confraternity of perpetual orison, praying the clock round, so that an unending stream of supplication should flow towards the Throne of Grace, will avail thee!"

The Chevalier remained prone. The voice changed from iron to brazen, ringing out like a trumpet.

"No, Tannhäuser! For what thou hast done thy soul is forfeit, thy body excommunicate, thy name anathema!" The pontifical hand, flashing with the emerald ring, rose, and seized the staff of olive wood, and shook it violently. "No! Sooner will this dry staff put forth buds, put forth green leaves, than thou be found worthy of forgiveness and thy soul redeemed from the everlasting pit where it shall go! Away, away! Wretched man, hideous lecher, sinner in excelsis, monster in human shape, child of Belial, Judas redivivus—away!"

Whereupon the miserable Chevalier, almost fainting, unable to move, was seized by two brawny monks and thrust from the room.

Chapter XVIII

OF THE MIRACULOUS BURGEONING
OF THE PAPAL STAFF

It was a month later, on a cold bright morning in January, that a pair of cardinals were discussing something in urgent whispers in a corner of the Vatican Vestibularium. Their heads were in apposition, their violet robes were agitated, their sapphire-ringed hands fluttered like ornamental birds. One of them held the papal staff of olive wood; the other was examining it with tremulous attention.

"Your Eminency bears witness to it?" said the first, the Cardinal-Presbyter of Santa Croce in Gerusalemme.

"'Tis even as Your Eminency reported," said the other, the Cardinal-Deacon of San Ciriace alla Terme Diocleziane.

"Should we show it to His Holiness, think you?" inquired the Cardinal-Presbyter.

"Or should we leave Him to find out for Himself?" murmured the Cardinal-Deacon.

But at that very instant the Holy Father himself appeared; this time he was dressed more simply, in the voluminous far-flowing petticoat of white taffetas and the surplice and pallium, with the pontifical stola and white house-cap. The cardinals fluttered forward in a swimming obeisance, and kissed his knee.

"There is something amiss," said the Apostle. "Your Eminencies, We desire enlightenment. Speak!"

With a quivering hand, the Cardinal-Presbyter motioned towards the papal staff standing in the corner. The Pontiff stepped forward, seized the staff and gazed on it; he turned pale, tottered and fell upon his knees.

"Me miserable!" he cried. "Behold these buds, these little leaves! A miracle!"

"A miracle!" and "A miracle!" ejaculated the cardinals, kneeling on either side of him before the magic staff.

Then the Apostle rose. His eyes were shining, his mien once more assured and imperious. "Amends, amends!" he cried. "Alert the sbirri, skirr the country round! Let not your faces in My sight appear, till ye have found that German Chevalier!"

But it is with infinite pain we must record that Tannhäuser had disappeared. The entire apparatus of the Papal constabulary was unable to uncover him. "He appears, Your Holiness," said the Cærimonarius some time later to the stricken Apostle, "to have vanished from the face of the earth."

And this was, in fact, precisely what had happened.

At the very moment when the Pontiff had first seen the budding staff, Tannhäuser was toiling up the Hill of Venus in the midst of a storm of many-sided sleet. He was in miserable case. His only garment was a piece of sacking, his feet were bare, and his hat, fastened to a string, had slipped on his back; incredibly gaunt and attenuated, limping like a cripple, he could barely crawl forward. Ah, what a change from his appearance in the same place a few short months ago, when clad in silks and satins, decorated with ruffs and rings and chains, he had minced up the how gloomy path of pebbles and dead lichen that wound between a wilderness of rocks! But with what tears of thanksgiving, with what a supplication of his thin fingers, did he once again survey the grotto, the vertical ellipse now crowned with twisted brown brambles.

Eckhart was sitting, as usual, just inside the entrance and out of the wet. "Well, so here you are again, eh?" he said, and laughed.

The Chevalier, giving no more than a terrible sob for answer, groped his way across the threshold for the second and last time.

The Return of Tannhäuser to the Venusberg

Chapter XIX

THE LAST

The Chevalier's bodily health was soon restored by diet and repose, but his spirits remained languishing, for he heard constantly in his ears the reverberant anathemas of the Pontiff and was quite assured he was irremediably lost. Alas! we who are more fully informed, know that a Plenary Indulgence was even then awaiting him in the Holy City. And we may ask, who will be held accountable for his backsliding on that day when all things are to be revealed? The office of judgment is difficult—nay, perilous; we dare not hazard even a guess. But pity 'tis that one should suffer through an earthly mistake of the Infallible, or be doomed to everlasting torment for a theological misunderstanding.

In the meantime, his wan looks and careworn air were quite out of place at the Court of Venus. The Queen herself, though constant in her efforts to cherish and cheer him, was secretly prone to admit he was becoming rather a wet blanket. Often, noting his absence from a dinner-party or masque, she had slipped away and found him forlornly mooning in some deserted grove or parterre, and seeing the tears on his poor cheeks had bewailed her inability to restore him to his former cheerful and epigrammatic self.

One evening she found him in more wretched estate than ever. He had crept away from a wonderful performance of Titurel's latest opera in one act *The Rite of Atthis,* where Spiridion was moving all hearts in the rôle of the inspired emasculate, and taken up his mournful station in the statue-strewn Garden of Dionysos nearby. His head was in his hands, his limbs drooping like those we admire in the figure studies of Mantegna, where the attitudes follow the languishing line of a dying flower. To the Queen's tender inquiry he at first gave only a heart-rending sigh; but at last he told the story of his adventures and the outcome of his pilgrimage.

"And so, Your Majesty," he concluded, "I am irretrievably damned, and the prospect is such that I cannot rid my mind of it. I have decided, therefore, to anticipate my torments in the only way open to me."

Venus was all sympathy and pretty puzzlement. "And how do you propose to do that, my dear Chevalier?" she asked.

"By putting an end at once, and with Your Majesty's gracious permission, to my miserable existence through the medium of a rope," he replied, and his face once more fell into his hands.

The Queen protested in the liveliest manner; but Tannhäuser was adamant.

Then she was silent for a while; her expression was still full of commiseration, only a little smile had begun to play around the divine lips.

"Well, if you really want to," she said at last, "we might make a kind of tableau of it, for Cas-

cabel's sake. Would you mind that very much,
darling? The poor fellow has been obliged to
execute frogs and mice and dummies for so long.
A real, human hanging would give him such pleasure, and it would be something he could look
back on for *years*—when he is by himself, you
know. I know just what he wants, and it won't
hurt at all."

Tannhäuser bowed an assent full of nobility and
resignation.

"You're a dear," said Venus, kissing him. "We'll
have it tomorrow at noon, then. I'll arrange everything."

The next day the whole court turned out for the
recherché spectacle, which was held on the fifth
terrace of the palace gardens. What a crowd there
was, and what wonderful toilettes and masquer-
ades everyone had devised! Lesfesses was notable
in a Chinese robe of yellow watered silk, wearing
a round pepper-pot hat, carrying a fan, and
mounted on high gilt pattens; the beautiful Mas-
carelle had disguised himself as a dwarf, and was
stunning in a suit of crimson broadcloth with bell-
like short pantaloons, a flat cap, a little silver cape
over his boss, and his stockings stuffed with quaint
knobs; Pimpant represented an embryo, and
evoked shrieks of laughter.

Around the scaffold was a select group of the
Queen's intimate circle. K— was there, as Colum-
bine; Farcy had gotten himself up as the Honour-
able George Selwyn, and was testing the mechanism
of the platform like a connoisseur; De La Pine
was in one of his most astounding dressing-gowns
figured like a San Benito; Mrs. Marsuple wore a
scarlet cap of liberty. Venus herself, sad, pensive

and resigned, was more beautiful than ever in a plain dark-blue cloak, a golden wig and a necklace of pearls.

Claude and Clair, still nude, wore little hangman's hoods of the loveliest, softest black kid; for they were to spring the trap, as a special treat, and so they wouldn't feel they were being left out of things. Opposite the scaffold was a special booth for Cascabel, where he reclined surrounded by his puerile entourage.

Everyone was in a flutter of anticipation as they waited for the arrival of the devoted Chevalier.

And there he was! The Queen's victoria, bearing him all alone, was already threading the serpentine avenue of the gardens; and now the Royal orchestra struck up the special Dead March which Titurel had composed the night before and whose sweet but triumphal solemnity immensely increased his repute as an improvvisatore.

The equipage was magnificent. The carriage, like some airy scallop-shell suspended over the delicate tracery of its wheels, was drawn by two lovely bang-tailed hackneys whose manes were twisted up in a row of little knots like pom-poms and tufted with snowy wool, and who stepped with all the daintiness conferred by shoes cunningly rolled and weighted. Curb was driving, of course; and with his jolly, bearded face beaming down from the box, in full ceremonial costume of dinner-coat, white tie and silk hat, his driving-apron tied behind him, holding the reins and the long-lashed holly whip in his fat, white-gloved fingers, he looked exactly like the 8th Duke of Beaufort as His Grace appears in the frontispiece to his book on *The Art of Driving*, in the Badminton series. And how handsome the Chevalier looked, bare-headed, in his white ruffled shirt with its low, rolled collar and full sleeves caught in at the wrists and fastened with diamonds, his black silk knee-breeches and stockings, and shoes buckled with silver flowers! There was a spontaneous buzz of applause as the carriage drew up beside the terrace.

The footmen sprang down and assisted him to alight. Pale but composed, he approached the Queen and bowed over her hand in respectful silence; then, escorted by Cosmé in cassock and bands, he mounted the steps to the platform. In the midst of a solemn hush he unclasped the twin diamonds at his wrists and bestowed them on Claude and Clair; then he stepped forward and addressed the gathering in a brief harangue, thanking them for their courtesy in assisting at the spectacle, touching on the pleasure he had found in their refined company, and concluding by asking for their prayers. This last request evoked a few scattered smiles, and Robinet was seen to cross his fingers, but when the Chevalier finished his little speech there was a general murmur of appreciation, for it was felt he had acquitted himself very well.

He stepped back, waving away the silken scarf which Cosmé proffered him, and as Claude lovingly adjusted the noose he folded his arms. Then, at a sign from Cosmé, Clair sprang the trap and the Chevalier dropped neatly through the opening, while Cascabel threw himself backward in ecstasy.

There was a great sigh from the concourse of spectators; then the orchestra struck up a tarantella, and the crowd began to disperse. Talking, laughing, complimenting each other, and flirting, they all trooped off to the Palace like a cloud of gilded butterflies. Claude and Clair cut the body down and laid it gently on the grass, and then they too ran off after the others. Venus alone remained behind, bending over the lifeless body of the Chevalier. As she looked at him her eyes filled with tears, and for a while she indulged the novel emotion of grief; for she found it interesting to place herself in the situation of a mortal confronted with the death of a dear one. But the novelty must have palled very soon, for in a minute or two she bent down and gave Tannhäuser a kiss on the lips; the colour came back into his cheeks, and he stirred and sat up.

"Where am I?" he said, putting his hand to his head.

"Why, where else could you be, but under the dear old Hill?" said Venus. "The fact is, my pet, there's no dying allowed here, any more than there is being born. We just go on as we are, and *I* think it's *much* nicer. Come on! it's almost time for lunch."

Tannhäuser began to laugh.

THE END

WORDSWORTH DISTRIBUTION

Great Britain and Ireland
Wordsworth Editions Limited
Cumberland House, Crib Street,
Ware, Hertfordshire SG12 9ET
Telephone 01920 465 167
Fax 01920 462 267

USA, Canada and Mexico
Universal Sales & Marketing Inc
230 Fifth Avenue, Suite 1212
New York, NY 10001, USA
Telephone 212-481-3500
Fax 212-481-3534

**Australia and
Papua New Guinea**
Peribo Pty Ltd
58 Beaumont Road
Mount Kuring-Gai,
NSW 2080, Australia
Telephone (02) 457 0011
Fax (02) 457 0022

New Zealand
Allphy Book Distributors Limited
4–6 Charles Street
Eden Terrace
Auckland
Telephone (09) 377 3096
Fax (09) 302 2770

Italy
Magis Books SRL
Via Raffaello 31c
Zona ind Mancasale
42100 Reggio Emilia, Italy
Telephone 0522-920999
Fax 0522-920666

**Germany, Austria and
Switzerland**
Swan Buch-Marketing GmbH
Goldscheuerstrabe 16
D-7640 Kehl am Rhein, Germany

Portugal
International Publishing
Services Limited
Rua da Cruz da Carreira, 4B
1100 Lisboa
Telephone 01-570051
Fax 01-352-2066

Spain
Ribera Libros S L
Poligono Martiartu, Calle 1, no 6
48480 Arrigorriaga, Vizcaya
Tel. 34-4-671-3607 (Almacen)
Tel. 34-4-441-8787 (Libreria)
Fax 34-4-671-3608 (Almacen)
Fax 34-4-4418029 (Libreria)

Wordsworth Classic Erotica